The
De...
Carousel

Also by Jeff Torrington

*Swing Hammer Swing!*

JEFF TORRINGTON

# The Devil's Carousel

Secker & Warburg
London

Versions of some of these stories have appeared
elsewhere, namely: 'The Poacher' in the *Glasgow Herald*;
'The Sink' in BBC publications; 'The Fade' in the
Scotia Bar Writers prize, and in the anthology
*Obsession* by Serpents Tail; 'The Night of the Worm'
in the *Edinburgh Review*; and 'Boag's Gallery' in
the anthology *Behind the Lines*.


First published in Great Britain in 1996
by Martin Secker & Warburg Limited
an imprint of Reed International Books Limited
Michelin House, 81 Fulham Road, London SW3 6RB
and Auckland, Melbourne, Singapore and Toronto

Copyright © 1996 by Jeff Torrington
The author has asserted his moral rights

A CIP catalogue record for this book
is available from the British Library

ISBN 0 436 20331 6 (hardback)
ISBN 0 436 20174 7 (paperback)

Typeset by Deltatype Ltd, Ellesmere Port, Cheshire
Printed and bound in Great Britain
by Clays Ltd, St Ives plc

## To

Margaret, who prevented the roof from caving in
while I laboured at the prose-face;

Jessie Bogacki, George and Janet Quinn
(hugely missed);

and the late Jim Leggat,
who gave Marshal Rommel such a hard time.

# Contents

# The Auto-Build Blues

Lissen, Mistah Ford,
You ain't stuck for room
Lyin there real easy
In your big fancy tomb.
Wisha had me a stick or two
Of nitro=g.
I'd blow you both t' Hell,
You'n your old Model T!

Yeah, tighten that bolt, bud!
Drive that screw!
You won't escape The Widow
Till she's had'r due:
That mean ol bitch
Ain't gonna grant you no spell
Till she's worked you to the bone
On the Devil's Carousel.

# Starting

Shoes in hand, each boozy breath cautiously drawn, mindful of the notorious creaking seventh tread, Steve Laker tipsy-toed up the dark staircase. His stealth paid off: he made it to the bedroom landing without disturbing the snoozing trio. It was an accomplishment that even the most experienced cat-burglar would've applauded, but he was only too well aware of what proverbially follows pride. His downfall was brought about by a fiendish trap set by his equally fiendish stepson, David, a repellent little toad with about as much warmth as an iceberg's asshole. This eight-year-old genius had pressed into service The Magic Egg of Proteus, which was just one of the many expensive and sophisticated playthings given to'm by his over-indulgent father, who was a big roller in the computer-games industry.

No sooner'd Laker's stockinged foot brushed against the toy than it went off like an exploding kaleidoscope, animating the landing's walls and ceiling with what looked like a whirling cloud of luminous confetti, while its percussion unit began a mad gonging and the image selector bleeped rapidly through its files. Suddenly, plastic petals snapped open around the Egg's upper surface, then from its dark, twittering heart, announcing itself with a baleful roar, there arose the fearsome looking Zorga – King of the Terrorsaurs!

The creature immediately got into its Lord of the Lizards routine, which included much pec-pummelling with its bright emerald fists while it roared louder than a colony of breeding walruses. Abruptly, the giant lizard fell silent, but it continued to pan its brutish head while its jaws opened and shut menacingly. Then, slowly, it sank from sight into the Egg's purring machinery. The monster's cessation of hostilities came too late for Laker, however, as the bawling emanating from wee Rachel's room indicated.

With a muffled oath, Laker groggily bent, intending to snatch the toy from the carpet, but he lost his balance and lurched against the banister, fetching his wristwatch a crack off one of its rails. Simultaneously, he lost his grip on his shoes, which, since Murphy's Law seemed to be operating on a full tank of mischief, went tobogganing all the way down the staircase to end up splay-footed in the light-dappled hall below.

As Laker staggered from the banister and again sought to get a grip on the din-maker – it was once more performing its *son et lumière* show at his shoeless feet – he was dazzled by a spill of light from their bedroom door. At the critical moment the cargo of booze he'd stowed away shifted and robbed'm of what little stability remained to him; gravity did the rest, and he landed in an undignified heap with his nose embedded in the carpet, just as Stella whipped open the door and stood glaring down at him. With'r hair infested with plastic rollers, and wearing a nightgown that was about as sexy as a shroud, she exuded more menace than a whole tribe of Terrorsaurs.

From'r mouth there flew the classic questions indignant wives have down the centuries barked at their late-arriving spouses, when like mobile breweries they come lumbering home: 'Where the hell've you been? Have you any idea what time it is?' Grateful that she hadn't carried'r adherence to the rules of this common marital confrontation to the length of arming herself with a stereotypical rolling-pin, Laker had begun dutifully to mumble token words of apology. Certainly, it wasn't expected of him to express his penitence for his late booze-besotted arrival by wallowing in an orgy of regret at Stella's slippered feet, one of which'd begun to tap impatiently at the unedifying and unmanly spectacle of her louse of a spouse grovelling on the carpet.

Within his skull, a Wall of Death rider began some warm-up laps, his speed gradually increasing until he'd become a vertigo-inducing blur. Closer'nd closer to the wall's rim the rider sped, each circuit driving Laker to a corresponding pitch of nausea, and with it the growing dread that if he didn't get back on his feet pronto, he was going to throw up on Stella's slippers.

By this time the smirking David had put in an

appearance. As Laker woozily assumed the vertical, the boy darted between Stella'nd him and, snatching up his toy, retreated to his bedroom, closing the door with a wicked slam.

Enter stage left the howling Rachel.

She was quickly scooped up into the secure haven of her mother's arms, an action that didn't deflect that good lady from unleashing a vociferous diatribe at her partner, who was groggily hanging on to the banister. During this high-powered harangue she let it be known to Laker, their neighbours, and to anyone still awake on the planet Saturn, that she'd had enough, thank you; that this was definitely the last straw; she was packing it in; leaving.

Still clinging to the banister (for some unaccountable reason its former solid oak had changed to a very stretchable rubber) Laker tried to get in an apology for his admittedly late arrival but she was having none of it. Her tone switched from verbal savagery to one of amazing tenderness as she sought to comfort the sobbing Rachel. After she'd managed to quieten the girl some, Stella resumed her cataloguing of Laker's character defects. He tried to butt in, to utter a few defensive words about the dangers inherent in leaving toys lying about in dark hallways, but immediately realised that this'd been an ill-advised move, about as clever as having a fly wee puff in a fireworks factory. Stella exploded. Almost incandescent with rage she scorched Laker with such a dazzling display of verbal pyrotechnics that he was convinced that had she been standing closer to'm she'd've scorched off his eyebrows.

4

Her arsenal of insults rapidly depleted, Stella drew a deep breath, enough air to fuel her final stinging remark:

'D'you know something – you're low enough to walk under a snake – without taking your hat off!'

This said, she abruptly turned and carried the snivelling Rachel into the bedroom. Its door thumped shut and Laker was left alone in the outer darkness, gripping the wobbly rubber banister.

About twenty minutes later Laker was to be found sprawled on his black leather armchair in the living-room. Although there was a bed in the spare room, it wasn't made up, and the very thought of digging out sheets and blankets from the linen cupboard made him feel dizzy. He figured he'd be as well to kip here for the night.

For a while he lay brooding on Boy David's treachery. There was no doubt that he'd deliberately set the trap. That he loathed the very sight of Laker was putting it mildly. Only this morning, at the breakfast table – Rachel in her high chair and Stella on her high horse (he couldn't recall why she'd thrown this particular moody. Maybe he'd coughed while she'd been describing the merits of curtain material, or he'd 'breathed sarcastically' while she'd being going into graphic detail about her really sinister headache) – the budding sadist had asked his mother what a parricide was. Stella, not wishing to violate her self-imposed vow of silence, had feigned ignorance and with a scarcely perceptible nod had fielded the boy's query to Laker. He hadn't responded for he knew perfectly well that the smirking imp was aware of the word's homicidal meaning.

Anyway, Laker had been busy re-reading a life-changing letter – a skimpy one-pager – that bore the logo of a Centaur and an illegible signature that looked like a pair of intertwined pythons either trying to screw or to chew one another. Tersely it'd informed him that his job application as a Telex Sequencer at Centaur Cars Chimeford Plant had proved successful. Accordingly, he was to report to the personnel office, Monday next at 8.30 a.m. prompt in order to rendezvous with the Senior Sequencer, Mr Stan Cutter.

Now seated in that black nightchair, wondering if grafting in a car factory wasn't too radical a step, he discovered that the crystal of his watch'd been smashed. Worse still, after he'd removed it he found that its innards had gotten bust too: its motionless digits were now only able to register the exact moment when he'd smashed the watch off the banister rail: 12:27. He gave it a gentle shake, willing its luminous digits to catch up with the scurrying world. But, like a frozen stellar system, 12:27 remained unmoved.

# Walking
# The Widow

A man who looked like a smudged hologram of Adolf Hitler sat on the edge of a desk in Centaur Cars' personnel office. He was on the phone, or, rather, the phone was on him, wedged between his chin and shoulder. To judge from his reactions, he was having his earwax melted by whoever was on the other end of the line. Steve Laker returned his attention to the mischievously amended notice that'd been taped to the ledge alongside the Enquiries push-bell: SING FOR ATTENTION, it invited. What might be an appropriate ditty? The American Depression dirge 'Buddy, Can You Spare A Dime?' suggested itself.

Laker eased his thumb from the nipple of the Enquiries pushbell. After some moments the window was drawn open by a youth with a scalpful of red hair that looked like a freshly pokered fire. 'What can I do for you?' he asked.

Laker handed'm the letter confirming his appointment as a Telex Sequencer at the Chimeford Plant. Having skimmed a glance across it the fiery-haired youth returned the letter. He was smiling although Laker couldn't see any justification for his amusement.

Someone else patently unamused was Adolf. Laker watched'm as he rose from his desk perch. His face registered more red blotches than were to be found on an old British Empire atlas, while his mouth fluently oathed into the phone. His telecon ended with'm literally coshing the cradle with the receiver.

Quietly chuckling, the youth flourished a hand in Adolf's direction, then, dropping his voice some, said, 'Steve, meet your gaffer – Stan Cutter,' to which, lowering his voice still further, he added: 'You've knocked it off – he's in one of his better moods this morning.'

At that very instant Laker'd been seized by an irrational urge to spin on his heels and start legging it to the nearest exit at a speed that'd make the Road Runner look like a tortoise on Mogadon.

The hangover he'd so recklessly courted the night before had been malletting his gourd like a manic xylophonist when he'd oozed back to demi-awareness. He'd found himself in the black leather armchair in the equally dark living-room, though, judging by how he felt, maybe dying-room would've been more appropriate. He groaned, as the sordid recollections began to dribble in. There was no dodging the prime fact – it'd all been down to him, the guilt was his alone. Yes, after a furious row with Stella (money, and their woeful lack thereof, had been the cause of their bickering), he'd stuck on his anorak and gone storming out of the house: destination – KARS lounge bar, his nearest boozer. There he'd gotten into the company of the zany pair, Laurel'n Hardy, Tommy Farr'n Dixie Donnigan, who all worked in the plant's trim shop. What a derisive roar'd arisen from them when Laker'd announced that he'd be joining them at Centaur Cars the very next day.

'Maybe I imagined it, boys,' shouted Donnigan, 'but I could swear I heard this gonzo claiming that he'd chop off his mitts with a rusty hatchet before he'd work for a multi-nat outfit – especially a Yankee one.'

'A shiny shoes number, eh?' said Laurel.

'A collar'n tie guy,' said Hardy.

'A "Down-Time" Dodger,' added Tommy Farr.

In the early-morning dark as the hungover Laker'd bestirred himself and groggily levered himself from the armchair, the very idea of becoming a car worker'd seemed so loopy, so bereft of commonsense, that he felt he would've been better to've checked into the nearest head-shredder. Certainly, being pilled to the gills with tranks and occasionally getting plugged into the mains had seemed to him, as he'd lurched into the kitchen to stick on the kettle, to've been a far more inviting prospect.

Cutter appraised him.

'So, you're the new piano-player?'

Cutter's voice was a wispy tattered thing but, considering he was a sixty-a-day man, and rarely let an hour go by without succumbing to his addiction for telephone tantrums, it was amazing that his sooty voice-box was able to reproduce even this hoarse utterance.

'Let's hope you're better'n the last fankle-fingers we had.'

Somehow Laker got the feeling that Cutter didn't seem over-optimistic about this.

'C'mon,' the Senior Sequencer rasped, 'I'll show you around the printer locations. Most of'm are in the Main Assembly Division, or, as it's better known – in MAD. We'll kick off in the prod/con office.'

They left the personnel building and, hampered by a scouring wind, fought their way across a weed-spored tarmacadamed yard and ducked into the prod/con's main entrance, where they paused to catch their breaths and to tidy their dishevelled hair. Cutter made do with a few finger-sweeps through his black'n grey peppered thatch, which was complete with Widow's Peak, longish sideburns, and a soot-smudge of moustache daubed on his upper lip. His hand was already dipping into his pocket for his ciggy case, but when he'd pushed a fag between his lips the Promethean wind kept plucking off the petal of flame that so briefly flowered at the lighter's fuel outlet. However, by recruiting Laker as a shield, Cutter eventually got the cigarette going.

'Where'd you pick up telexing?' he now asked.

'Eurocables – a small telegraph outfit.'

'Bagged you, did they?'

Laker frowned. 'What makes you think that?'

'Think what?'

'That I'd been sacked?'

'Well, were you?'

'The firm folded.'

'So you decided to grab the shark by the sore end, eh?'

'Sorry?'

'Don't you read past Page 3 in the papers, then?'

'Not with you?'

'This company's about to go belly-up, that's what.'

A black binbag, crackling and snapping in the wind, swooped by, an event that Cutter, with a 'told-you-so' nod, seemed to be implying was a metaphorical confirmation of his prediction.

Laker shrugged. 'They've been saying that since Noah felt the first raindrop.'

Cutter'n him'd gone into the office, where he was given a low-key intro to some of the schedulers and analysts with whom he'd liaise from time to time. Scott Wainbeck, who wore a blue shirt with white stripes, and had a pink head with bald stripes, was, to his obvious displeasure, delegated by Mal Kibbley, the prod/con Martian, to show Laker the ropes regarding the office telex machine, while he took the pensive-looking Stan Cutter back with'm to his office. In a matter of seconds the Martian could be heard verbally tearing yet another strip from the Senior Sequencer's hide. (Martian, Laker was to learn, was a nickname bestowed upon the factory's top management by KIKBAK, a slag-rag that was both clandestinely published and circulated within the car factory.)

The sulky-looking Wainbeck led Laker to the office's teleprinter: it was stuck in an alcove near a window that looked out onto the wind-lashed yard, where now not one but three binbags were to be seen cavorting.

The teleprinter, he was glad to see, was a T15, the same model he'd used back in the old cable office. They stood for a minute or so watching the machine's oscillating carriage, and hearing the rhythmical drumming of the typehead on the paper roll. Whoever was broadcasting from the distant end was a dandy telex op, a Super-Sender as they'd called such fast-fingerers back'n Eurocable. Although he was himself no slouch at the keyboard, he nevertheless felt pangs of inadequacy when faced with such slick sending. But maybe it wasn't human telexing at all; it could be that the broadcasting printer was hooked into a loop of perforated Murray tape that functioned automatically, being a technological cousin of the Pianola.

However, Laker'd soon to discount this theory when without any diminution, neither in speed nor in sending rhythm, the broadcast sequence was interrupted by about half a dozen line-feeds after which the following cryptic message appeared:

Alb go 2 ax mach. COOP.
Take fm 43 2 49 (0905 GMT)

Wainbeck had to be asked before he deigned to tell Laker that it was an instruction for Albert Ackroyd to take a supply of telex rolls to the axle printer since it was COOP, i.e. Completely Out Of Paper. Copies of the broadcast from items 43 to 49 were also required.

And who was Albert Ackroyd?

Again Laker'd to do the asking.

Ackroyd, it seemed, was a sort of freelance

sequencer whose beat was confined to MAD. A kind of troubleshooter, he was always to be seen hurrying like the proverbial blue-arsed fly from one crisis to the next; his prompt action had saved many a mis-sequenced car from getting blacked by The Widow's ops through his timely substitution of the appropriate paperwork for the rogue body.

Laker taxed Wainbeck's patience still further by putting another query to'm. The scheduler sighed. ' "The Widow's" a nickname for the main assembly track.' Taking advantage of a pause in the telex broadcast, Wainbeck tore off about a yard or so of the printout from the machine and spread it across a nearby table.

Laker's curiosity re The Widow was not yet satisfied. He put another question to the decidedly sniffy Wainbeck, who, having separated the three-ply paper sheets, taped them now to the tails of the previously broadcast items.

'It's fairly obvious,' said the huffy looking Wainbeck. 'There're so many guys conking with ticker shutdowns or brain blow-outs that the local hospital here calls one of its wards The Centaur Recovery Unit.'

Wainbeck took up a live broadcast roll. 'As you can see,' he said, unfurling it, 'triple-ply rolls are used on this printer; the same applies to those in MAD, which throws you spare copies to cover machine breakdowns or overprints. By the way,' added Wainbeck, 'don't depend on the punters to bother their arses about letting you know that their printer's on the blink;

believe me, those buggers wouldn't crack on if the bloody machine was on fire!'

With this remark, the scheduler, whose unfathomable hostility towards him had, if anything, increased, spotted Cutter leaving Kibbley's office and, abruptly, without so much as a simple 'cheerio' to Laker, went stomping back to his desk.

As they passed through a series of storage areas on the way to MAD, Cutter filled him in on some more of the telex sequencer's tasks: 'You broadcast to seven stations: the harness section; axles; gearboxes; wheels'n tyres; engine drop-point; prod/con office; and the seats section – it's across the road in the trim shop, by the way.'

As they approached the main door at MAD's southern end, Cutter paused. 'The most important thing to keep'n mind, Laker, is that mistakes cost: if you screw-up, then the ops follow suit; make a balls of the line-sequence and the car-shells'll start to boomerang. Another thing, don't be fooled by The Widow's apparent slowness. In fact she's fairly spanking along. Fifty cars'n hour she builds, which, believe me, isn't bad going for a multi-mix track.'

As they moved on again, Cutter asked him if he'd heard of Murphy's Law. Laker nodded. 'Well, take it from me,' growled the Senior Sequencer, 'this is where the bugger lives – Murphy, I mean. Make one balls-up'nd there's just bound t'be another pair of boo-boos at its back. You can depend on it.'

Cutter'n the new-start entered MAD, the Main Assembly Division. He'd half-expected to find himself in a locale that was modelled on a Dantesque vision of

Hell, perhaps one of its more torrid circles, a place that throbbed with unceasing uproar, and where the restless phantom-like shadows of pillars, posts, and hordes of teeming humans were projected onto dense, vaporous clouds. The contrast between his conjectured picture of MAD and the reality now confronting him couldn't've been more marked. Instead of flame-laced infernal visions and Chaplinesque exaggerations of the tyranny of machines, Laker had a sensation that paralleled his first scuba dive when he had sunk, truly awe-stricken, through panicking shoals of jewel-like fishes onto the coral reef's iridescent floor, the optical areas of his brain all but fusing at the startling visual novelties that continually presented themselves. It'd be absurd for him to claim that MAD offered similar eye-boggling glories to those available in tropical lagoons. But, nevertheless, there was an abundance of startling things to be experienced there. For instance, car-shells, painted in a wide variety of sparkling hues, cataracting from the cavelike mouth of the transfer tunnel and swooping down onto The Widow's long reef, which was populated with myriads of white boilersuited ops. The car-shells pouring into MAD carried with'm the acetone smell of nail polish, and the sounds to be heard were many'nd varied, from the rappings of hammers and the softer impacts of wooden mallets to the tortuous whining of power-drills, the almost constant honking of forkies' horns as they darted along passageways formed by store-stows.

As it passed from station to station each shell picked up the necessary components, beginning at the harness section where the car's wiring system was installed. It proceeded on its convoluted journey around tight bends and through aerial chicanes, until a long time later, now heavily burdened with axles, gearbox'nd engine, wheels and tyres, seats and the thousand and one accessories that transform a chunk of painted metal into a fully functioning machine, the car was carried by The Widow's possessive metal arms onto the Final Line, the last build stage to be negotiated before the ingenious assemblage, the product of many hands, could truly claim carhood. Soon it reached the roll-off ramp, where, after getting some go-juice splashed into its tank, it slipped The Widow's clutch, its engine was fired, and an op drove the car from the ramp to its assigned storage area.

In all, their tour of MAD took about forty-five minutes to complete. During the course of it, Laker'd been given intros to many rednecks, greybacks, and ops, the names of whom he'd mostly forgotten by the time they'd arrived back at their starting point. Cutter had explained that the term 'Rednecks' was derived from the crimson-collared overall which senior foremen wore to differentiate their rank from the all-grey garment of the greybacks (junior foremen). Shortly before this they'd bumped into the troubleshooter, Alf Ackroyd. There was a Toby Jug look to'm, a belt-stretching gut, stumpy legs, and bodyguard eyes that clocked and assimilated the source and cause of any movement up to a radius of ten feet from'm. But this mobile eye-balling mostly ignored Laker, only pitching a glance in his direction when Cutter introduced them: his hand gave Laker's a cold little tap, then vanished up his sleeve again. He certainly bore out Wainbeck's blue-arsed fly simile, for throughout the half-minute he stood with them his feet stirred restlessly, plainly indicating that this introduction was forestalling some car-saving mission.

Although Cutter'd mentioned the possibility of car damage on the build tour Laker hadn't been surprised by his lack of reference to the damage inflicted upon men and women by having to repeat the same actions over'nd over. True, Wainbeck'd referred to heart attacks and strokes but he'd said zilch about mental injury. It was true to say, however, that most ops he'd seen on the tour hadn't looked particularly stressed or harried as car after car, with an almost mesmerising slowness, slid past them. But not for a single moment, as he'd trudged alongside Cutter in this industrial cavern with its muted sounds and its colourful queue of drifting car-shells, was he fooled into believing that modern car plants were humane places, and that they rated concern for their workforce as a prime considera-tion. Yeah, they could tell that to the Marines. But there wouldn't be much point in telling it to the veteran press shop workers – they probably wouldn't be able to hear you.

No, to give credence to the preposterous notion that there was such a thing as a humane car plant was only a step away from accepting the tyrant's claim that his regime was a benign one because at executions his firing squads always fixed silencers to their weapons.

Laker began to wish he'd acted upon his earlier intuition to cut'n run. But for some reason it seemed too late for such drastic action. Anyway, if he was to be honest with himself, he doubted now whether he'd have the courage to flee.

Cutter led the new-start to a flight of steel steps which gave access to the transfer tunnel. It looked like an elongated aircraft fuselage with opaque wire-meshed windows set into the walls about every five yards or so. These plus roof strip-lighting provided illumination although the tunnel remained gloomy. It also felt frigid, the floor exuding a metallic coldness. To their left flowed the long procession of car-shells, accompanied by polythene wrapped seats, while on their right empty slings, their track wheels clattering, returned to the trim shop.

It seemed odd to Laker as he recalled that beneath them was a main road along which traffic busily passed. This thoroughfare bisected the plant, possibly making it unique, and had led to a press reporter describing Centaur Car Company as a factory that suffered from 'industrial schizophrenia': in other words one half didn't know (or care) what the other half did. As they clumped along the metal passageway, Cutter occasionally stepped into the car-shell flow to examine the specification tallies, or, as they were better known, the 'spec tallies'.

Approaching from the tunnel's distant end came two uniformed security men, who, Laker had also learned that morning, were referred to throughout the factory as snipes.

Both security men paused every now and again to point roofwards, the shorter of the two jotting into a thick notebook.

'Get ready to salute,' murmured Cutter, nodding at the factory flatfoots.

'Who are they?' asked Laker.

'The taller one's the Supersnipe or Security Chief, known to one and all as Twitcher Haskins.'

'Why Twitcher?'

'Because he's one of them nutters who'll lie in a wet ditch for hours spying on birds. The other one's Mark Steeley – he'll shortly be taking over the Supersnipe's number from Haskins, who's retiring.'

They met up with the officers about halfway along the tunnel. Haskins – he'd gaunt features and an austere-looking mouth – eyed Laker with his custom-ary suspicious glower as the Senior Sequencer intro-duced him. Steeley seemed to be far more affable and had a noticeably warmer handshake. He indicated his notebook.

'Tell me,' he said to Cutter, 'what do you think of the possibility of installing security cameras up here?'

Cutter shrugged his lean shoulders.

'Not much,' he replied. 'The Magpie'd probably nick'm ten minutes after their installation.'

Laker grinned.

Laker, about to say something, was interrupted by a dismissive Haskins: 'Rubbish, all that's needed to choke off this thieves' highway is an old-fashioned pair of padlocks.'

'You still for having the tunnel locked then?' queried Cutter.

'It's the best answer,' said Haskins.

'High time we caught up with modern security devices,' said Steeley.

'Install one camera and in no time the things'll be sprouting all over the Plant like damned toadstools, which'll mean a non-mobile security force, men sitting on their asses screen-watching,' Haskins snapped.

'How are my lads going to gain access to the Southside if you've padlocked the Tunnel?' Cutter wanted to know. 'I mean the telex crew have to sometimes check out printers.'

'They can go via the exit gates.'

'But what if it's raining?'

'Then they'll get wet, won't they?' replied Haskins.

At that moment Cutter spied something wrong on a line. A spec tally was missing from the Mermaid Green Super Salamander. He immediately darted to the follow-up car-shell, seized the paperwork which was taped to the bumper and whipped it clear. He shouted for Laker to join'm.

'What did I tell you about Murphy's Law?' He held up the spec tally. 'D'you see what's happened here?' He peeled the tally from another to which it'd adhered.

Laker, who hadn't a clue what his gaffer was on about, said nothing.

'That daft bass Biggles has got them stuck together: chances are that the Salamander's not been telexed. Here, take this to Sam Gates in the telex office. Get'm to check if it's been broadcast. I'll tie up with Alf Ackroyd.'

'Where is the telex office?' Laker asked.

'To your left after you get down the steps, now hurry!'

Haskins and Steeley had moved on.

Cutter sped past them on his way back to MAD

while Laker proceeded to the trim shop. He'd have no difficulty in recognising the telex office for the previous night in the pub Laurel and Hardy had described it to'm. It was, according to them, an office for which no expense had been spared.

'Last word in plushness, I'd call it,' Hardy had said. 'Thick-piled carpets, mahogany timbered walls, modern furnishings, chairs your arse will sink into. Everything, in fact, but effing chandeliers.'

On descending from the transfer tunnel Laker found himself caught in a deafening uproar of shunted carshells, bell ringing, a racket to which a fitter repairing a paint trolley added more decibels with a heavy hammer. Laker'd to raise his voice to shouting pitch before the tradesman latched on to what he was asking. The man jerked his thumb towards a dilapidated structure which seemed to've been constructed from old bread boards and roughly nailed wooden spars. Its roof consisted of wire mesh and was poxed with plastic coffee cups, yellowing newspapers and ripped copies of old *Centaur Lines*, the company's official inhouse magazine, and some tatty copies of the renegade KIKBAK.

Laker figured that this must be the seat section's telex point Cutter had mentioned. Going into the stone-floored shack he was startled to see a man in a grey coat overall with wavy, grey-flecked hair who sat with his back to'm, busily and speedily operating a telex machine.

'Excuse me,' said Laker, 'can you direct me to the telex office?'

The man swung round and appraised Laker. 'You're standing in it, pal.'

Lakers' jaw dropped. 'You've got to be joking!' he exclaimed.

The man shook his head, a slow smile gathering on his lips. 'You're the new guy, eh?'

Laker nodded.

The telex op rose from his rickety chair and pumped Laker's hand. 'Sam Gates. And you?'

'Steve Laker.'

'Well, Steve,' said Gates, 'they haven't rustled you up a locker yet but feel free to hang your jacket from the air conditioner.' He pointed upwards at the wire-meshed roof.

Never mind his jacket, at that moment Laker felt like hanging himself from the roof.

ISSUE 97    KIKBAK    A LAFFING ANARKIST PUBLIKAYSHN

The following poem was written by the "bard of Chimeford" We
publish it as a timely reminder of the dollar-driven credo of
the Multi-Nationals: " Profit requires no self-justification!"

### THE COMING OF THE CENTAURS.

Where cars stand now
There once grazed cows,
And 'hairy engines'
Pulled the ploughs:
As close to heaven
As the Lord allows,
That was Chimeford
Before the Centaurs came

I watched them comi g
O'er the headland
With all their smoke
Andthe muck and bedlam
Now there's no peace
At night in bed, man,
With Centaur din.

They soon destroyed
Our village habits
Their neon-lipped women
Bred like rabbits
Fresh gang blood, for
The "Sentor stabbitz"
- Street Broncos,

They demolished, too,
Our well-loved bars:
"The Clipper'nd "The Plough'nd

Stars."
Replaced'm with a wine bar
And a lounge called 'KARS.'
A licensed garage.

Most nights I pray
Till early dawn
Crying Centaur devil's
get thee gone'
And take with you
Your horseman spawn
Back whence ye came!

# Night
# of the
# Worm

'What's it mean if your feet swell up?'

'Dropsy,' Butcher said without hesitation.

'Dropsy?'

'Means you're filling up with water – starts with the feet.'

The warning bell rang, and the stand-clear lamps flared.

They stepped back from the Salamander they were working on. It was a buggy-shunt line; the trucker's machine punted it forward two trolley-lengths. They moved with their car down the line. When the shunt stopped they resumed their positions.

Wormsley leaned over the Sal's bonnet to pump-screw a grille cover into place. Next, he went round to tap some grommets into the car-base holes assigned to'm. Butcher drilled bezel fix-points. He flicked the long airline every few seconds to stop it from fouling the trolley wheels. He poked his head into the car-shell. 'My granny died from dropsy,' he said. 'I was at her bedside when she drowned.'

Wormsley drew a length of twine from the bundle dangling at his belt and secured the near-side door. The Worm, as he was sometimes referred to on the trim-line (though never in his hearing), looked like a man nature had concocted when it'd been in a real bitchy mood: it'd begrudged him stature; misaligned his jawbones; planted a joke nose on his sad clown face, and then, before it'd posted off to the world this parcel of mischief, it'd franked him with a strawberry-hued birthmark.

Wormsley moved to the next car, a basic Sultan. From the grille-cover rack he selected a matching colour, then raked in the canvas bag strung around his waist for the washers and securing screws. Beneath a long spine of fluorescent tubes, in a section about eighty yards long, over two dozen boilersuited operators were scrambling around, darting between, leaning upon, and crouching within the car-shells, each of them adding to the uproar, whether it was with drill, mallet, hammer, screwdriver, or the sound of their own upraised voices. Supplementing this bedlam was the heavy rattle of metal wheels on the concrete floor as the truckers locked their machines onto the laden trolleys being jettisoned from the paint shop, then propelled them with jarring shunts down the adjacent storage lines. Another din-maker was the glass section, from which there frequently arose the sound of breaking glass as an op (usually a greenhorn!), who'd yet to master the art of malletting glass, smashed through it and was forced to endure the ignominy of loud derisive cheers, not only from his mates but also from the ops who manned the headliner section, which shared the same line as the glass ops.

'It's more the left one,' Wormsley explained. 'Took me all my time to get the blessed thing on – my shoe, I mean.'

'You've probably got what they call Sinister Dropsy,' said Butcher as he came across to Wormsley's side of the car.

'Sinister Dropsy?'

Butcher tugged his airline clear of a spilled bucket of trolley clamps. 'Yeah, read about it in the *Reader's Digest*.' Butcher's drill whined fiercely as it bit into the metal. 'How's your left hand?' he shouted.

Wormsley examined it. 'Seems okay.'

'Looks a bit puffy to me.'

'No, don't think so.'

Wormsley scooped a handful of grommets from his bag. He shouldn't've brought up the subject: already bugs of pain were swarming down his left arm.

Butcher ducked his head into the car. 'Heard about this bloke, like yourself, he couldn't get his daisy roots on either. So he goes to his quack and tells'm his feet've swelled. It turned out, though, he was more'n need of a woolhead than a sawbones.'

Wormsley's carmine brow registered a rising graph of bafflement.

Butcher grinned. 'Bugger-all wrong with his feet. Y'see, while he was on the nightshift his wife'd been tig-toying with a fancy man. And, one morning, does he not quit her boodwar with the wrong bootsies on his tootsies! D'you get what I'm driving at?'

An estate-line shunt, being made by Basher Bradleigh and, as a consequence, a real eardrum-cracker, left Butcher's mouth flapping to no account. Immediately afterwards the trim-line bell shrilled and the stand-clear lamps blazed. The burdened trolley wheels began to rasp and grind over the screws and the washers that choked the floor rails. Wormsley tracked his car body. He stepped carefully around oily patches and automatically ducked the airline that swung and writhed overhead like a flail. As he selected a grille cover, Matt Gunnion, the section's relief man, arrived on the scene. He made a snapping motion with his hands and the nodding Wormsley passed to'm his canvas bag and pump screwdriver. As he secured the bag around his waist, Gunnion peered curiously into Wormsley's blighted features.

'You okay?' he asked.

'What d'you mean?' Wormsley looked thoroughly alarmed.

Gunnion flipped the screwdriver into the air then caught it. 'You look a bit "nightshiftish", that's all.'

As if worry'd got into his workings and reduced his gait to a fankled trot, Wormsley hurried from the section. As he did so, he accidentally elbowed a bunch of bonnet-stays, which cascaded onto the floor. An operator shouted angrily but by then Wormsley was skirting the dodgem-car uproar of the storage apron, heading into the vinyl-roofing section. Here, in its comparative quietness, a glue-pump's piston rose and sank with shiny sighs.

Wormsley made for the toilet, passing into an area of frenzied activity, where buggies herded car bodies into brilliantly-lit pens, and forkies, their horns honking imperiously, bustled up'n down the passageway. On an overhead track a half-dozen black Super Sultans were passing like a funeral procession.

Wormsley paused by a noticeboard. Behind its cracked and dusty glass a few sheets of paper'd been tacked. His scrawny neck stretched like a chicken's as he squinted up through the streaked glass. The blurred image of a fish swam into his teary gaze. This, he decided, must be a notice to do with the plant's angling club. The sheet next to it bore the familiar Centaur insignia, so it was probably a letter from the company. The final notice wasn't illustrated – just letters milling like ants on the creased page. Wormsley pressed a hand to his chest. His heart had begun to behave oddly, leaping and skipping like a salmon on the rocks. His left foot was trying to get into the act as well, vying with his heart for attention. It felt as if the shoe he'd had to literally force onto his foot as he'd dressed for work that evening was at least a size smaller than when he'd removed it. Such a sudden shrinkage wasn't possible, Martha his wife'd claimed, and she should know about such things since she was the manageress of the shop from which she, herself, had purchased these selfsame shoes. His present discomfiture must therefore, she reasoned, arise not from the shoe but from the foot itself. For some reason it'd become swollen. If the condition persisted he'd have to seek medical help. Meanwhile, since she'd thrown out his old shoes and she wouldn't allow'm to put on his expensive dress ones, then he'd just have to grin and bear it. Well, right now he might be bearing it but he certainly wasn't grinning.

As he was about to enter the toilet, a pair of wet-deck ops came stampeding from it. One of the men was wagging a papertowel under his nose, while his mate, who looked urgently in need of oxygen, managed to utter a single name in passing. 'Skunky!' he croaked. This proved warning enough for Wormsley, whose limping detour took'm from the building out into the pallet-storage yard. Skunky Scanlan was notorious for the stench he made when he occupied a skunkbox. He could even outstink Curly Brogan, whose fecal odours had earned him the nickname of King Pong.

As Wormsley crossed to the pallet-stacks, a fine web of rain broke on his face, and a cat, at one with the night, except for its sulphurous eyes, sped across the puddled tarmac. He relieved himself in a sour corner and was just on the point of emerging from the stacks when a huge pain opened like a firework in his chest, crackled ominously in its cavity for some seconds, and then spluttered out.

He sagged against the damp pallets, taking in great gulps of wet air. Indigestion! 'The bends', as some of the regular nightshifters called it. He'd have to get a powder or something to settle his stomach. Best to see to it right away.

The old joke about how to find the sick bay: 'Die noisily, at least twice!' occurred to Wormsley as he saw the green cross symbol above its entrance. Beyond this door was a dim waiting-room and – according to another gag – an even dimmer nurse.

The waiting-room furniture was on the sparse side, consisting as it did of a couple of benches, and a scattering of steel-framed, canvas-bottomed chairs. The walls were painted a puce colour and were smothered with safety posters. One of these posters had a photo of this punter, who'd had the foresight to wear industrial eye-protection, grinning smugly from a head that looked like a broiled pumpkin.

The waiting-room had an occupant, who, going by his clobber – boilersuit, wellingtons, and rubber gloves – was a wet-deck operator. He was slumped on one of the benches, his legs spread, chin dug into his chest, and his face concealed by a baseball cap. He was motionless, and remained inert even after Wormsley, with a light cough, signalled his presence.

Through in the surgery the nurse's voice could be heard. It soon became obvious that she was on the telephone. What became even more apparent to Wormsley was that her conversation was dealing, not with the disappointing outcome of some medical intervention, but, of all things, the failure of a knitting pattern to achieve its advertised promises. It was typical. they could be dying out here – that bloke on the bench looked like he'd already snuffed it – and all she could think about was knitting patterns. Wormsley began to cough loudly. Even then the wet-deck operator didn't stir. Through in the surgery, though, Wormsley's bronchial outburst was having the desired effect – the nurse began to wind up her frivolous chit-chat; the receiver went down, then came the soft tread

of rubber-soled shoes on the surgery's parquet flooring. Preceded by her shadow the nurse pushed wide
the door.

'All right – who's dying?'

It was sarcasm with a smile. She stood in the
doorway, a young woman with red hair, wearing a
white coat overall. She padded back into the surgery.
The thought of jumping the queue occurred to
Wormsley but he dismissed the boldness of the notion,
even if two persons – one of them asleep – didn't
constitute a real queue in the normal sense of the word.
He'd no guarantee though that, the moment he began
to tip-toe past him, the snoozing man wouldn't
suddenly metamorphose into a fiend with a mouthful
of bone-splitting oaths. Wormsley approached the still
figure: 'You're next, mate.' He reached out a hand and
shook the op's flabby shoulder. Almost immediately,
the man's head rolled from its pivot and dropped with a
squashy thud to the floor. Simultaneously, the torso
seemed to melt, to gush away from the grasp of the
astounded Wormsley, dissolving into a heap of clothes,
which consisted of a baseball cap, boilersuit, rubber
gloves and wellies.

The dummy's head'd been fashioned from a punc-
tured football, its body from cottonwaste and rags.
Wormsley couldn't have explained his next actions:
instead of leaving the collapsed dummy where it was
he'd been unable to overcome the compulsion to drag
it from the waiting-room; odder still, he did so with a
furtiveness that suggested he'd been involved in the
prank. He left the thing propped against a bin, out
there in the soft rain, having – even more bizarre! –

taken the trouble to rejoin the head to its torso, topping off his useless activity by the replacement of the peaked hat.

Normally, even if you hopped into the surgery carrying your own leg, the Centaur medics had but one panacea – an aspirin. If, however, the would-be patient made a convincing job of passing out once or twice in the surgery itself, they'd been known to grudgingly issue the odd sick-pass – a matter of small comfort to its recipient for it was a virtual death sentence, proof to the sick person that he or she was suffering from something that was undoubtedly terminal.

That the nurse actually intended to physically examine him came as a worrying surprise to Wormsley. She peered into his grey strabismic eyes, then sank a bright thermometer into the dental squalor of his mouth. Next, seizing his skinny wrist, she took his pulse. Near panic seized him when the nurse reached for the blood-pressure apparatus. She affixed the canvas sleeve around his arm then began to inflate it. The resultant reading seemed to bother her. His blood pressure was too high, she informed him. She plucked the thermometer from his mouth but this time made no comment on its reading; she kept this info to herself. Very well, then, two can play at that game – he wouldn't tell'r about his swollen left foot. What's more, he'd debar himself from thinking about it, which would be one in the eye for that smartmouth, Butcher. All that malarkey about lovers limping home through dawn streets in the wrong footwear. Wife-pinchers and toe-pinchers. He might've smiled at his tame little joke if the nurse hadn't chosen that very moment to give'm some even more worrying news: he must lie down for a half hour or so, to see if his blood-pressure stabilised. She'd contact his section foreman and put'm in the picture.

In a semi-dark room which housed a bunk-bed and a heat-treatment lamp, Wormsley lay on his back and did exactly what he'd been told by the nurse not to do – he worried. Why'd she asked what his phone number was? He hoped they didn't intend to disturb Martha. She hated having her sleep broken. In fact, she'd insisted that he should go on constant nightshifts because she found his snoring to be insufferable. 'Like a hog trapped in a wind-tunnel!' was how she'd described it.

Tightly clenching his eyelids, Wormsley sought to visualise his sleeping wife, tried to hear the sound of her light breathing, to smell her fragrance, but the various intimate details refused to gel, wouldn't focus. There was a sinister exception, a clear-cut image of a pair of shoes, walking along by themselves, but he immediately suppressed it. His eyelids resettled on skewed orbs. His heart seemed to be limping – there was no other way to describe it: limp-dub . . . limp-dub . . . limp-dub . . .

At the back of his brain something was stirring, something was growing. The narrow bunk creaked under Wormsley's restless movements. What kind of nonsense was this? Had the nurse slipped some sense-sliding stuff into'm? Might it take him into a long swoon from which he'd never return? His eyelids flew open, and his gaze, thirsting for the prosaic, gulped in great draughts of it: lamp . . . flex . . . socket . . .

windows . . . glass . . . walls . . . posters . . . bunk . . . blankets . . . man . . . feet . . . hands . . . fingers . . . blood . . . veins . . . arteries . . . heart . . . limp-dub . . . limp-dub . . . limp-limp-limp-dub . . .

His composure partially restored by the common-place, Wormsley's thoughts drifted back to his child-hood. Bully-bait, that's what he'd been – a human punchbag. His classmates had called him Wormy to his face, and had rarely missed a chance to stick barbs into'm or to walk on his very treadable body. One sadist had even suggested cutting him in half to see if the divided ends would wriggle. Adolescence was purged in a heap of soiled memories, and he'd insinuated himself into adulthood, creeping from one lowly job to the next, eating the dirt. He might've continued on this downward spiral, tunnelled to the very heart of failure itself, if a dowdy thrush called Martha hadn't spotted him with her beady eye.

After what seemed much longer than half an hour the nurse came to him with her blood-pressure appara-tus. His condition had not improved. In fact, if her expression mirrored the pressure-gauge, then it'd considerably worsened.

'I'm sending you home,' she said. 'Give this to your own GP.' She handed him a sealed envelope. 'You must see'm at the earliest. D'you understand?'

Wormsley nodded. Something equivalent to 'And you shall be taken to a place designated, and there be hanged by the neck until you are dead . . .' had just been pronounced, yet there he was, nodding meekly, even trying to look apologetic for causing her all this bother.

The Company estate car, bearing the Centaur emblem on its white flanks like an exotic brand, sped through the wet pre-dawn streets. Wormsley sat in silence, irked by his driver Billy Sloane's attempts to trawl an evasive pop-music programme from the radio's shoals of static and Morse bleatings. Eventually, he abandoned his search, snapped off the radio then, sitting back with a sigh, took the full measure of his seat. Both men stared out into the amber dazzle of the sodium-vapour street lamps, where the floating rain was laying its gloss on every object it brushed against.

Familiar landscapes swept into view.

'This'll do me,' Wormsley said.

Sloane shook his head. 'I'll take you to your gate.'

'No, drop me here. Best not to disturb the neighbours.'

After the car had made off, its tyres swishing juicily on the soaked tarmac, Wormsley lodged his lunchbox under his arm and began to limp along the pavement. As he trudged past his own avenue he looked longingly in the direction of home, but, despite the increasing agony of his cramped left foot, his resolve remained intact: Martha's sleep must not be disturbed!

He was plodding along now like a deep-sea diver, many fathoms deep . . . air running out. A slab of rock seemed to be crushing his chest. He felt himself being sapped of energy, as if somewhere in that heap of gore and bones he called his body a sluice-gate'd been left open.

Soon he was forced to slump down onto the damp step of a fishmonger's shop. At the pavement's edge stood a bin, encrusted with fish-scales: its death-stinks corrupted the early morning air.

Wormsley placed his lunchbox beside'm on the step, then, panting hoarsely, reached down and wrested the shoe from his stinging foot. The relief he felt was so overwhelming it amounted almost to bliss. He turned the shoe between his hands then, summoning up his dwindling resolve, he angled the shoe so that it caught the light from the overhead street-lamp. Taking a deep shuddering breath, he peered inside.

From his clenched blue lips a groan forced itself and, as yet another fireworks display opened within his labouring chest, he hurled the shoe from'm; by sheer fluke it clonked into the kerbside bin.

'Give that guy a coconut!'

It sounded like an old man's voice, but by then, Wormsley, his brief moment of light already extinguished, was tumbling unseen to his appointed resting place.

## CASSIE NO MORE SHALL CHASSIS

A Special Report From Ace Scribe - Newsy Parker


The loss of Cassie String - the Chassis-Plate mid-shifter
brought expressions of deep boredom to the faces of Union
leaders when someone happened to mention it during a game
of stud poker in the Watertank Hut.

"It all happened so suddenly,' said her former workmate,
Lavina Laffinstok, when I dropped by their portakabin to
express my condolences. On a shelf stood poignant mementoes
of the well-liked Cassie - her shaving mug, her Luger Pistol,
and her stuffed Clydesdale horse. Cassie's co-worker - the
dashing bald Irish colleen, Eliza Snitchencasser, kept herself
occupied by dropping lighted squibs into the hopper of the
plate-making machine.

Lavina shook her head: 'Poor kid, she's taking it bad.'
Aware that I was intruding during a moment of private grief,
I begn to tiptoe out. Softly the wot-eyed Lavina called me
back. 'What about the sheet, punk?' she rasped. 'Aincha got
no sheet?'

'What sheet?'

'Whacha - some kinda retard? The sheet  for our middy,
that's what.'

'Sorry, I know nothing about a sheet.'

'Dig this  dope!' Lavina laughed harshly.

'Don't mind her,' Eliza whispered. 'It's the sudden loss,
you see.'

I nodded. 'It's okay. I know all about post rheu matic
stress.

Something hard dug  into my back. 'What's this?' I
asked.

'It's a gun brimming with bullets, Bub!,' Eliza snarled.
'So, make with the sheet, creep, or I'll transplant your
ticker!'

'Give it to'm anyway,' panted Lavina. 'Swtch a light on in
his guts ...'

Luckily, at that moment, their gaffer entered and both
women rushed to knit'm a Fair Isle cardigan.

I came away sadly  aware of how  grief can distort humans,
make even the most sane into barbaric basket-cases. Cassie's
stuffed Clydesdale whinnied in protest, so I guess I'd best
include the Centuar. You got that? No damned horsemen, stuffed
or otherwise. After all, I gotta retain some plant cred ...

# Send
# in the
# Clowns

Laurel and Hardy, a right pair of comics, were veterans
of the troupe of industrial clowns that was dispersed
throughout the plant from the press shop to the
rectification area. It was all but impossible to find even
one section that lacked its clown or practical joker.
Trapped like their fellow-workers in the pitiless geo-
metry of the circle, prisoners, too, in the tortuous
orbiting of carousels large and small, they maintained
their sanity with laughter, even when they found
themselves being drawn in and devoured by the very
rollers'nd teeth of Henry Ford's gift to mankind – the
Assembly Line.

'Let us forthwith dispense with the wasteful folly of
bringing the assembler to the parts; rather, let us bow
to logic by bringing the parts to the assembler.'

Gee, thanks, Henry – you're a spiffing sport, you really are!

On the trim-line Laurel and Hardy were door-handle fitters. So long had they been doing this job that they performed it automatically, and, as a consequence, had the time to exploit their mutual talent for comedy: joke-telling, leg-pulling, or just fooling around in general. They'd become an act, a continuous cabaret-on-wheels staged amidst the thunderings of shell-storage line shunts and the clamours arising from the trim-line itself, which every few minutes was biffed forward a couple of trolley lengths by a trucker – a rowdy operation preceded by flashing orange warning lamps and strident bell ringing. Undeterred by these painfully high-decibel operations, both Laurel and Hardy used mime when speech was inaudible and packed as many words as possible into any fragments of silence that occurred, although, as Hardy put it, these were as sparse as bibles in a brothel.

Oddly enough, the hilarity that morning centred on deafness. It seemed that on the previous evening the comic pair had taken their wives to the Centaur's Social Club. Before setting out Laurel and Hardy had fibbed to their respective spouses that the other woman who'd make up the foursome was hard of hearing, and to compensate for this by addressing her with a raised voice when they conversed.

Once in the Club and seated at their table, the wags had winked to each other as both the women had begun to bawl pleasantries. The louder one yelled, the more decibels her companion piled on, until it sounded like they were having a good going rammy

42

instead of a chat. Eventually, a Club committee member, looking decidedly embarrassed, approached Hardy and asked him if he would mind asking his lady guests to speak more quietly. Hardy nodded, then, making shushing noises to the mortified women, had said, 'Drop the volume a bit, ladies, there's been a complaint from Ben Nevis that you're causing avalanches.'

Laurel had nodded, 'That don't surprise me none, I thought maybe your missus was a bit Mutt'nd Jeff.'

Hardy'd laughed. 'Deaf? My Mildred? No way! She could hear a snowflake landing in Red Square – couldn't you, honey?'

It was equally possible that a keen-eared Muscovite could've heard Mildred Hardy's brolly thumping her spouse's cranium. Certainly, everybody in the Club heard it, even old Joss Drayton, whose eardrums had been cratered by a decade in the press shop – and he'd been in the games room at the time watching his cue shot racing to a smacking collision with a pool-ball pack. Something analogous to the exploding triangle, the many colours caroming off each other, had been simultaneously occurring inside Hardy's head as striped and dotted elements of his consciousness cannoned brightly on the dark blue baize of his mind, while others scurried into pockets of lapsed awareness.

'And as if the lump on my noddle's not enough to be going on with,' Hardy said as he fingered his skull, 'doesn't yon wee bugger Charlie Hazelhurst, you know, the doorman, try to get his oar in demanding our club cards and threatening us with instant execution. He'd to be sent packing by the other stewards and told to look after his own patch, which Charlie being Charlie was reluctant to do.' His audience, who'd been chuckling at Hardy's tale, was scattered by the trim-line shunt bell, but each operator carried off a private grin as he or she tried to imagine what the outcome had been on the practical jokers.

But as it happened they weren't to find out until a considerable time later, for just then, Dixie Donnigan, the dayshift steward, who'd been attending a meeting of the JRC (Joint Representatives Council), arrived back in the section. He was the bearer of bad news: Henry (The Worm) Wormsley was dead. After the miracle of being granted a sick-pass on the nightshift he'd been found dead on the step of a fishmonger's shop near his home. Apparently he'd suffered a heart-attack.

'Why outside a fishmonger?' Hardy wondered aloud.

'And why was he singing a hymn?' asked Laurel.

'A hymn – what hymn?'

' "Nearer My Cod To Thee," of course,' said Laurel.

## A BUNGLE IN THE JUNGLE!

Wet Deck op, Chorlton Cum Hardie
has been disqualified from the
SEMOLINA SAFARI CONTEST.for
alleged public indecncy.Hardie
who won his place in the
Contest by accurately estimat
ing the exact amount of lumps
to be found in an average
platefull of edible grout the
canteen refer to as semolina.
Hardie who was strongly-
fancied favourite, is claimed
by Safari monitors to have in
the middle of the steamy
jungle seen the British cont-
estant doing a pee in his
helmet in full view of three
female contestants which
caused them such dismay that
they were unable to continue.
Said a disconsolate Hardie:
Itth all a nathy mithtake,
How wath I to know that a
a pith helmet wath for keeping the thun off? ...

## LET IT ALL HANGOUT!

There's a very red face to be
found amongst the Martians-
the fizog in question belong
ing to none other'n Elmer
'Fudd' Franx, Centuar's top
UK design manager. It seems
our Elmer got lifted while he
was 'walkingthe dog' up on
Hooker Heights -the arresting
officer was a Dalmation call
-ed Murphy who happened to be on
the spot working a stake-
out on a fake pooper-scooper
scam. When he observed the
accused 'Wagging his profits in
public.' A barking-mad
Elmer strongly denying the
allegation claims that he'd
merely been .'Loosening his
bills ...' Should the case
come to trial, Elmer plans to
plead the so-called "Hot Ash
Amendment" that grants the
accused the right to remain
silent on the grounds that it
might incinerate him ...

## DIE ASBESTOS YOU CAN, PAL!

Those punters who work in F
Building where disturbing
amounts of asbestos have
turned up, need not be
unduly alarmed about health
risks - they should be
bloody terrified! The fact
that our dear 'Dr
Mengeles' has described it
as the 'Less letnal white
stuff' should be warning
enough! Watch out for more
colourful evasions ...

## WOT A HORSE LAFF!

As a creature
It's just a farce,
Who was its inventor?
It shits from its mouth,
And talks through its arse,
I think it's called the
Centaur!

# The
# Sink

Curly Brogan had an idea: the bones of it was that he'd
fake his own death.

'I like it so far,' said Frank Jordan, his deputy
steward. They were lounging against the storage-yard
wall, having a puff A bright morning, sun loose in the
sky like a runaway cartwheel, tawny spokes of light
glancing everywhere. Tarry odours rising from their
white underseal-spattered boilersuits. Out here nothing much doing in the way of work: Midge Stacey – all
four feet of'm – was forklifting car-shells onto the
loading platform, where a hoist gang leisurely transferred them to paint-trolleys; over by the water-tank
The Sleeper was fixing himself up with a cardboard'n
foam-rubber sunbed. Brogan's mucky thumbnail
scraped a blob of underseal from his hairy forearm.
Toadlike, lenses of sweat quickening in the rough folds

of his face, and his baggy body leaking odious guffs, he was not a man to get downwind of. Most of the squad kept him at arms' length, though they did send'm to croak on their behalf at union meetings; Brogan was a croaker of distinction in that shrill swamp.

He removed his blotched baseball cap and vigorously scratched his hairless dome.

'What d'you think, then?'

'Bout you being dead?' Jordan took a saving draw on his skinny roll-up. The thought of this two-hundred-weight bag of shit dropping into a hole appealed to him. For a start, he'd no longer be plagued by the man's brute stinks – his aftergrave lotion, as the underseal squad called it. Another boon would be not having to listen to all that Marxian crap Brogan was forever braying. If there really was a spectre haunting Europe then a whiff from either of Brogan's armpits would soon exorcise it. On the other hand, as a shoppy, the man was really indispensable. What other steward could strike terror into the Martians merely by the approaching tread of his unwashed feet?

Jordan took another half-draw on his ciggy. 'Tell me about it,' he invited.

It seemed that the tenant who rented the apartment beneath Brogan's had been sent home, incurable, from hospital. 'Liver's like a chunk of cardboard,' Brogan explained. 'An alky. Telling you, if they cremate 'm, he'll burn for a fortnight!'

With a scattering of blond sparks Jordan's cig stub spun away. 'I'm still not with you.'

'It's dead simple.' Brogan grinned at the accidental pun. 'The bloke I'm on about has the same handle as me. No relation, mind, just the identical name and address. Used to work in the small parts. Got bagged for overdoing the bevvy. With me now?'

'Just about.' A pulpy cough bubbled in Jordan's chest and soon he'd to turn his head away to spit blackly. He wiped his lips with a linen rag. 'When this neighbour of yours pegs out, say today or tomorrow, it'll get around it's you who's croaked. Right?'

Brogan nodded.

'Then, I suppose there'll be a notice in the snuffer columns, and that'll put the tin lid on it.'

'Pine lid, you mean.' Brogan dropped, then heel-screwed his cig butt. 'He'll be a gonner by tonight. Tea's definitely out.'

They watched The Sleeper as he tried out his sun-bed, laying his long stark body on the yellow foam-rubber. A private plane with white lettering on its cherry wings and fuselage passed daintily overhead. Its pilot would probably think he was flying over the Centaur Car Company, located at the old village of Chimoford, a molecule of link on the map, its claim to mention being the well-authenticated birth of a two-headed bull there in the year of our Lord, 1884.

Like the Martians the pilot of the Cessna aircraft was at too great an altitude to see what really went on at ground level in this industrial asylum, this mechanised madhouse, where adults on the nightshift played infantile games like 'Film Stars' or 'I Spy . . .' while, right now, one of their dayshift counterparts seemingly found amusement in pretending to be dead!

'You mean you'd be willing to drop dough for the sake of a crummy hoax?' Jordan asked.

'I told you, I'm down for unpaid leave-of-absence.'
Brogan showed a gobful of rotting teeth. 'The boy's
wedding's in Torquay, remember?' His freshly-lit fag
crackled as he sucked happily on it. 'A good lad is our
Patrick – none better. He's going to meet all the
expenses for the missus and me – rail tickets, hotel bills,
you name it. He wants us to make a mini-hol of it. Bit
early in the season for deckies and donkies, I suppose,'
chuckled Brogan. 'But I dare say I'll find a cosy little
alehouse with a bookie's scarce half a furlong away
from it. And while I'm getting to know the fella at the
payout window like he was my own brother, sure
mother'll be doing her rounds of the shops.' He
nodded. 'She's hellish fond of a bit potter around the
shops. "Window-shopping" she calls it, though I don't
recall'r havin' bought a perishin' window yet.' He
laughed and slapped his thigh. 'No, nary a single
pane . . .'

The Sleeper stashed his sunbed behind some empty
oildrums, then with his robotic gait came marching
across the yard.

'Frankenstein walks, eh?' said Brogan from the
corner of his mouth. 'A bolt through his neck – that's
all the bass needs.'

They each gave a nod of acknowledgement to the
sombre-faced giant as his shadow fell on them but he
went past as if they were stains on the wall and entered
the building. Brogan and Jordan followed a few
moments later, walking beneath The Widow where it
formed a loop to carry its paper-shrouded car bodies
from the underseal booth along the demasking grid.
The burdened cradles rocked as they negotiated the

tight bend, and from the cars' freshly-sprayed undersides a black rain fell on the tarpapered floor.

Before ducking into The Hole, Jordan paused to tighten the muslin rag about his neck, jockeyed the mouth-mask into position, then pulled up his boiler-suit hood. He took the gun from Ted Rawlins, the section's relief man, who moved quickly away, obviously glad to get out of the underseal booth's tarry tomb.

With the pumps behind him beating out their unflagging rhythm, Jordan assumed his spraying position: feet apart, head held up and slightly canted, a stance which eventually played hell with his dorsal system. A Centaur Sultan body closed over his head like a lid. He raised the gun's nozzle and with sweeping motions began to spray the tape-masked underside with sealer.

Through the booth's tarry slit he could see Brogan jawing to Dixie Donnigan, a trim-line shoppy. As a demasker, Brogan had one of the cushiest numbers in the squad, his job being to rip off the tape that'd been slapped over boltholes and other orifices to prevent underseal-fouling. Donnigan soon departed, having, no doubt, acquired the longing for some fresh air. Brogan continued to crop masking tape, tossing it in sticky black lumps into a wastebin. Jordan went on staring at'm and, eventually, the senior shoppy, becoming aware of this scrutiny, grinned in return then, raising a gauntleted hand to his chest and making his short legs wobble, he mimicked a heart-attack. Maybe he would've had a genuine one if he could've tuned in to his deputy's masked curse: 'Go down, you bastard! Go down for real and let me out of this craphole!'

That night Jordan dreamed about Brogan. He saw him, armed with a ripped butterfly net, go staggering through a grove of turpentine trees that showered him with a hot black resin. He was chasing a cherry-coloured moth which had tiny white death-heads etched on its wings, but it fluttered an elusive yard or so beyond his uselessly swooping net. Jordan, watching from behind a tree, saw that Brogan, still totally intent on the capture of the moth, was in fact running into quicksand. A shouted warning would've been enough to've saved 'm but Jordan remained silent. The frolicking moth became a humming bird that lured Brogan further into the quicksand then hovered on purring wings over his bald head as it vanished beneath the choking mud. From the bird's throat there issued a stream of flute-like notes . . .

Jordan groaned awake as his wife's elbow dug into his back.

'Who can it possibly be at this time of night?' she asked.

Jordan switched on the bedside lamp then sat up with hurting eyes. A slimy cough began to unwind in his chest as he reached for the chirruping phone.

'Hullo.'

Brogan's voice boomed in his ear: 'That's some bark you've on you. Should see a vet.'

Jordan frowned. 'D'you know what time it is?'

'What's time to a dead man?'

'You pissed or something?'

'Just a wee rehearsal for the boy's wedding.' Brogan's tone changed, 'I'm giving you this bell to let you know everything's fixed.'

'Fixed?'

There was a swallowing sound followed by Brogan's heavy breathing. 'That's right. Just fall in line, y'know, play it as it falls. Hullo, you still there, Frank? Hullo . . .'

Another conversation had broken into the circuit. It soon collided head-on with Brogan's to produce a pile-up of wrecked sentences: 'Hullo . . . Who's there? . . . Is that you, Malcolm? . . . Get off the line . . . funeral . . . I'm trying to . . . crossed line . . . Hang up at once, d'you hear? . . .'

Jordan obeyed the curt instruction, clamping down his receiver before lifting it again and clattering it onto the bedside table. He dragged back the covers and got out of bed. His wife spoke to him as he shoved his feet into slippers. He shrugged. 'Nobody. Just a mate. Drunk.' He went through to the bathroom and spat into the lavatory pan, then, coughing all the way, he trudged downstairs to find his roll-up tin.

The next morning, five minutes before The Widow was due to stir, Jordan stood by the card table jiving a teabag in his mug. As always at this a.m. he felt rough. Very growly. Knowing this, most of the men steered clear of him until the first hour had passed. Gus Gebbie, though, paid no heed to such mood niceties. His morning face abrim with news, he came at the trot into the underseal section and headed straight to Jordan. 'I suppose you've heard,' he began.

'Shag off, Gus!'

Gebbie, as usual, was unabashed. 'It's about Curly,' he said.

Jordan slung the sapped teabag into a bin. 'What about'm?'

'He's a gonner! Cerebral haemorrhage. His brother phoned me last night.'

The news of Brogan's sudden 'death', accelerated by Gebbie's genius, was all over the plant in less than an hour: from the underseal section to the paint shop and paint hospital, thence into the body'n white, and the press shop, it hummed like black electricity, penetrating Broadmoor, whose militant ops, egged on as usual by The Human Sardine – the senior block steward, who made the media ogre of some years back, Red Robbo, look about as menacing as Liberace in a diamanté-studded boilersuit – had immediately advocated a down-tools show of respect. The Human Sardine rapidly changed his mind about this, however, when informed by the framing shop's senior Martian, Tony Briggs, that his men's respectful gesture would take place off-the-clock, in other words it'd come out of their paypackets.

The news about Brogan had already reached the machine shop and the die'n jig section, while The Widow carried confirmation of Curly Brogan's 'demise' into MAD, through messages sprayed on the car bodies' protective paper wrappings: 'CURLY BROGAN, R.I.P.' The internal telex system also broadcast the news and it ran in thrilling tributaries

54

into the harness section, seats, axles, wheels'n tyres, gearbox section, engine-drop-point and rectification area. It even reached Siberia (the sales compound), where misty denizens could be seen from afar checking, so the rumour went, birds' nests in the unsold cars sector.

An unexpected bonus came Jordan's way – he was transferred from The Hole to the 'late' Curly Brogan's former demasking number. Now, as he stripped tape and chucked the soiled croppings into a bin, he found himself doing something that, given the circumstances, showed a marked lack of respect – he was whistling while he worked!

Hearing his name being called, Jordan glanced down from the grid. Two men stared up at him: Tombstone Telfer, a redneck, and Tommy Stevens, the section snagger. For a man who believed smiling caused cancer, Telfer's face for once bore an unexpected glimmer of gladness. It wasn't too hard to figure out why; most foremen Jordan had met that morning had worn the same secretive smirk on their clocks.

At first, handling responses to Curly's 'death' had been a botheration to Jordan. All those crappy clichés as they dropped from this or that mouth – 'He'll be missed . . .' 'Can't get over it . . .' 'Looked as strong as a puggy . . .' 'You never know the minute . . .' – had irked him. But after an hour or so attitudes began to normalise. 'I hear Curly's undertaker's claiming "dirt money",' said big Guy Guyler, with that side-mouthed drawl of his. Somebody else had it about that the local sewerage works was flying its flag at half-mast. There was also a story to the effect that when he'd learned it was Brogan he'd been called to see, the priest had tried to phone in the Last Rites.

Stevens took over the demasking; then, with a choppy head movement, Telfer signalled for Jordan to follow him. Walking a pace or so behind the redneck, Jordan met up with the Irish Sweep, a broom-pusher whose brain, it was said, was being mailed to him by instalments. 'Is that right about Curly?' he asked. When Jordan confirmed the news he shuffled his big grey boots and said: 'I hear it was a terrible haemorrhage.'

'A cerebral haemorrhage, Michael.'

'Aye, terrible right enough . . .'

Aware of Telfer's impatience, Jordan moved on. He got a friendly wave from McQuirr, who worked at the seats-lift section, and Naughton over in the repairs bay mimed his awareness of Curly's demise by pinching his nostrils, then drawing a finger across his throat. The foreman, as Jordan had anticipated, led'm to The Byre, an office which, built mainly from glass, always looked too fragile to house the turbulent personality of Ted Bullock, or, as he was more generally known, The Bull.

As they came into the office, Bullock was making one of his theatrical phone-bawls, punching words into somebody's eardrum with his nailgun mouth. Brogan claimed that this was merely a ploy used by The Bull to intimidate stewards as well as greybacks; in reality he was bawling down an empty line. He used other psychological props, such as the chair Jordan was being waved towards, a shabby, rickety affair in comparison to the plush upholstered throne on which the trim shop superintendent was lording it. There was, too, the framed photograph of Bullock receiving a warm-looking handshake from the Company's president, George C. Warrender, at the Paris Motor Show when Centaur'd launched the Salamander range. Another telling touch was the large blue ashtray on the boss-side of the desk compared with the coffee-jar lid that'd been placed at Jordan's disposal.

The phone receiver made its expected crash-landing, and The Bull addressed a few remarks to Telfer about the stock depletion ratio of velour seat trim for the Sultan Super Estate, then, running a finely sharpened pencil down figure columns on a computer print-out, he very gradually brought Jordan into focus.

'Sorry to hear about Brogan,' he said, lounging back in his ritzy chair. 'How old was he?' When Jordan told'm he cocked a silvery eyebrow. 'Took'm for fifty, at least.' He stroked his grizzled hair. 'It's this place – puts years on you.' The phoney patter continued for a few minutes longer: hypocrisy humming to itself at the graveside, masking its smirk with a hankie. It was funny to recall that the subject of all this fakery was probably sitting, right now, half-smugged in a Torquay-bound train.

'Listen, John,' The Bull addressed Jordan affably, though inaccurately, 'this business leaves a couple of things in the air, if you catch my drift. Now, the way I see it –' Jordan started to interrupt him and The Bull held up an acknowledging hand. 'Yes, I'm aware of that. But this is purely informal. Right now, as you say, you're only temp shoppy, but, from what I hear, your

57

becoming full rep's a formality. So, let's take it as read. Tell you what I'm after, John . . .'

And he did, while Jordan let his words slide through his head. Brogan's hoax was becoming like that variety act in which the performer sets a series of plates spinning on rods, then dashes from one to the other in order to preserve its motion. It was obvious that sooner or later some part of the joke would wobble beyond control, then the entire farce would come tumbling down.

The Bull droned on. What he was after was peace and harmony in the underseal section. Certainly, Mr Brogan had only been doing his job, but recently things had got so tight that, well, a sparrow couldn't shit on the underseal roof without a block meeting being called. It was time to stop the confrontations.

At this Jordan sat up a little. Could he perhaps sniff a deal in the air?

Later, that afternoon, Jordan was sitting in the trim shop snack area, having a smoke and a coffee. It was a rowdy spot: there was the usual din from the nearby seats section; the gruff horns of forkies as they plied to'n fro in the passageways; and, closer to hand, the gab of operators enjoying a respite from the tracks. At his elbow, Spunky Madden was doing one of his card tricks, and a bunch of men craned over him, watching his every move. Familiar with Madden's jiggery-pokery, Jordan paid only scant attention to the card manipulations. Someone else, even less concerned, was The Sleeper. He sat at the far end of the table, back against the wall's cream paint, his face as usual visored with sleep. What went on inside that shuttered head?

Was this zombie stuff just an act, and all the while behind his lidded eyes thoughts were whirling faster than Madden's mesmerising hands, conning them?

Jordan glanced up. Two senior stewards, Ron Yardley and the portly Alf Cross, were nodding to him as they approached. They parked themselves opposite him and lit fags. Yardley grinned (Cross didn't) at the chirrups from the adjacent tables: 'Watch it, lads – it's Trotsky and Potsky! Must be important – they're fuck'n moving!'

Cross, whose nickname, Double, was a well-known sarcasm, wasted no time in coming to the point. Scarcely allowing Yardley more than a minute to lay a small verbal wreath for Brogan ('A good man to have on your side . . . Got mucked into the Martians . . . Dependable . . .'), he leaned aggressively towards Jordan. 'You were in The Byre this morning, s'that right?' Jordan nodded. Cross's cigarette stub died with a hiss in a coffee puddle. 'The Bull trying you for size in his back pocket, was he?' He shook his head. 'Bloody waste! . . .'

Yardley, who looked faintly embarrassed by his partner's vehemence, tapped some cig ash into a used coffee cup. 'We hear you've got Curly's job already. S'that right?'

My, my, the T & G tom-toms had been busy!

Jordan flipped the lid off his roll-up tin. He began to tear out some rust-coloured shag. 'Job goes with the territory. You should know that. Makes it easier for the shoppy to get to meetings and so on.'

Yardley nodded. 'Y'see, Frank, when a new shoppy happens along the Martians sometimes hand out lollipops. Y'know, to sweeten'm up. That's why it's a good time to screw a favour from the bastards.'

'I already have.'

Jordan ran his tongue along the roll-up's adhesive strip, then massaged the cigarette into shape.

'D'you know what they're giving us?' Both stewards waited expectantly. When he told them, their jaws twitched.

'A sink!' Cross said. 'A fuck'n sink!'

'With an electric urn,' Jordan added, savouring their dismay. He tapped the loose shag-strands into the ends of the roll-up. 'They're going to whip out the cracked sink and replace it – top priority. Be able to have a wash-up in the section now.' He lit his hand-roll. 'We never could get Curly interested.' Jordan grinned and blew smoke over them. 'Well, you know what he thought about soap'n water.'

The stewards, looking slightly dazed, left him.

Spunky Madden nudged Jordan then passed to him a piece of paper. It was a cartoon, obviously the work of Leroy from the wet-deck. It depicted Brogan's burial, the coffin surrounded by a crowd of mourners, each of them wearing a gasmask, as was the officiating priest, who was reading the funeral oration from *Das Kapital*. Ghosts from adjacent plots could be seen whizzing off with hastily packed suitcases, fingers held to their spectral noses. In the foreground one worm was saying to another: 'We've got a ripe one 'ere!'

Jordan laughed and returned the drawing to Madden. Shortly afterwards Donny Morton from the inspection booth stopped by with the good news that the facilities men were already in the underseal section checking out the new sink's location.

'You're some kid,' said Madden. 'Brogan for stinks – Frankie boy for sinks!'

Someone had crowbarred Brogan's locker and gutted it. Missing were his teapot, caddy and sugar box. Also taken was his much-thumbed copy of *The Ragged-Trousered Philanthropists* and an unknown quantity of porn mags. The oncoming dayshift ops mostly shrugged when they heard of it: locker-screwing wasn't uncommon. Anyway, what good was a teapot to Curly now?

'Probably the porn-hunters,' Archie Gilpin, the section's comic, said as they stood around the rifled locker. 'They'd know Curly liked a bit of tit.' Jordan and the others nodded. Brogan's red-hooped tea mug lay minus its handle on the concrete floor, amongst a litter of union bumph and scattered playing cards. There was also a pair of frayed and greasy looking baseball boots. Gilpin gingerly toed one of them. 'Bet these bastards walked back by themselves.'

With a murmur of laughter the men began to disperse.

Jordan stooped to gather some of the union stuff but he made a point of ignoring the baseball boots – there was, after all, a limit to one's loyalty. He grinned as he closed over the locker's buckled door. When El Stinko did his Lazarus, when he returned from the grave, he was not going to be chuffed about this. A smirk creased Jordan's lips. Tough titty, Comrade Shitty.

Standing by his own locker, getting into his boiler-suit, Jordan was approached by Vic Logan, the mirror-shift shoppy. Usually good for a joke, even after a ten-hour stint on the demasking grid, Logan looked sombre this morning. Odder still, he didn't want to discuss the theft while in the locker-room. Jordan agreed to go with'm out to the loading bay. On their way there, as they skirted around paint trolleys that cluttered the floor, Jordan got a pleasant surprise – for the first time in the history of the Centaur Car Co. a plumber'd actually been working on the nightshift, a rebuff to those cynics who claimed that the nocturnal leak-brigade spent the dark hours playing at Brag beneath an upturned tub. The obsolete sink, its back broken, lay on the floor like an enormous set of dentures: its stainless-steel replacement was already bolted to the wall.

'Nice work, by the way,' said Logan. 'McCandlish says he'll send a spark round this morning to connect up the urn.'

On the loading bay they lit up cigarettes. Beneath the platform in the grey yard there was the noisy coming and going of workers, nightshift flowing through dayshift, and beyond them, the frantic bleat-ing of horns from Calamity Corner, the punters' carpark. As he took his first drag on the cigarette Jordan puzzled over Logan's odd behaviour. Brogan's hoax had been sussed – was that it? Somewhere, a little night bird had twittered and the walls of the joke had come tumbling down.

Logan began to quest . . . no, not to question'm – there was an underlying rasp of interrogation to his tone. Jordan nodded to his first query: That's right, he'd been late in leaving the plant yesterday. He'd been attending a safety committee meeting. 'Cyril Coogan had a dose of the verbal skitters. Just couldn't get the bastard to clam up. You know how he can be when his north'n south starts to – what? In the locker-room? Me? After the meeting, you mean? Yeah, sure I was. Had to get out of my work rags, hadn't I? Y'see, my neighbours think I'm a bank manager.' Jordan grinned, but Logan's next question wiped all traces of amusement from his face. Had he seen anybody lurking around the locker-room while he'd been changing his clobber? And, had he happened to notice if Curly's locker had been intact at that time?

'Fucksake, Vic, what gives? You're not suggesting that I'd anything to –'

Logan was shaking his head. 'Course not, Frank. No way. I'm just trying to pinpoint the probable time of the break-in. Y'see, there's more to this than just another locker bust . . .'

Sometimes, for the squad's amusement, Spunky Madden put on a conjuring show: eggs became apples; paper flowers volleyed from soup cans; coins were snatched from the air. And all of this mystification unfurled itself on a stream of patter without which, it seemed, the machinery of the con would seize up and spit out its dry bearings. This very thing was happening now as Logan's next words were blasted by the man-your-stations klaxon. Jordan strained to hear.

'The snipes found what?'

'A couple of car radios,' Logan repeated.

'In Curly's locker?'

63

Logan nodded.

When Brogan's rifled locker'd been discovered by the oncoming nightshift, security had been alerted. While examining the locker's contents the snipes'd found two radios wrapped in one of Brogan's old boilersuits. The thief, or thieves, had apparently shied away from touching anything that'd been worn by Curly.

'The silly bastard!' was all that Jordan could find to say. He repeated it, his fierce draws on his cigarette sowing sparks in the gloom. Out in the yard stragglers were hurrying into their respective buildings, and through the wall Jordan could hear the underseal pumps starting up.

'I suppose even though he's snuffed it they'll still raid his flat,' Logan said.

Jordan nodded. Twitcher Haskins, the Supersnipe, well known for his messianic zeal, would go all the way to Hell for a windscreen wiper. No doubt he'd get the civvy fuzz to do the job, and it was on the cards that they'd raid the wrong flat and go blundering into the cancer victim's gaff: You rake the box, Charlie – I'll frisk the widow! It'd all come out in the wash soon enough. Brogan was beyond union aid now, a cert bagging case. Curly, himself, never defended a thief, he simply pulled the plug on'm. He could scarcely hope to be the exception to his own rule, could he?

Later, Jordan stripped soiled tape from freshly undersealed Salamander and Sultan car bodies which The Widow delivered to him at the rate of fifty per hour. So repetitive were his actions that his brain soon switched to auto-pilot, freeing his mind to wander where it willed. He found himself recalling a paragraph Curly Brogan had read aloud to'm from one of his lefty books – another of his irksome habits. How'd it gone again? Yeah: 'The Capitalists are the tomb robbers of history . . . they . . . they steal forth to prise . . . No . . . they steal forth in the night to prise open the door of that . . . chamber wherein . . . something . . . something . . . Democracy, was it? . . . blah, blahs its fateful sleep – and lets Curly Brogan's porn get heisted by a creep!'

Jordan grinned at his facetious amendment. The klaxon blared and The Widow stopped. As he came down from the grid, Spunky Madden took Jordan by the elbow. 'You're wanted, Frankie boy,' he said. 'C'mon.' He led Jordan towards the loading bay. Most of the squad had assembled there. 'Clear the way!' ordered Madden, and the group parted to reveal the gleaming sink, complete with steamy urn.

Madden handed Jordan a small bar of soap. 'Right, Frank, do us the honours.'

Jordan, grinning at the men's derisory cheers, stepped up to the sink. He turned on the tap and a robust gush of water soused the steel. Dipping his hands into the flow, he palpated the soap. Spunky Madden began to laugh and so too did the squad, their hilarity swelling even more as with a soft oath Jordan turned and sheepishly held aloft his black stained hands.

BIG HOIST SCANDAL AT CENTUAR (CHIMEFORD)

Electric Yo-Yo Men's Secret Contingency Plan Exposed!

Alerted by rumours that hourly-paid punters are being
victimised by Liftmen, Kikbak responded by sending a
reporter on a look-see mission. Disguised as a Butcher's
apron, and balancing a board of baps on his noggin, our
man stepped smartly into the Southside's canteen's lift
and barked: 'Follow that cleaner - don't lose'r!'
    The yo-yo man, surfacing briefly from his coma, tried
bravely to fight off a yawn. but kiseed-the-canvas
between floors, then puckering his lips sought to lay a
smacker on the lift's celling, when our man board-bapped
the pervert.
    For seourity reasons we cannot name our reporter
Zack Debronski for the simple reason that his dull
parents stuck'm with the boring handle:- John J. Dyookars
(-pronounced by'm as'Duckarse to get his own back'on his
folks). Dyookars, who
is being man-hunted ( not to mention bloodhounded) by a
cracked Interpol team for trafficking in parsely.,
quickly locating a secret compartment in the liftman's
balaclava he fished out a piece of paper which was
badly snotter-stained which prooved that the cryptic
message had been written by someone with acode in their
nose. At the risk of having refined old ladies spitting
through our office letterbox at midnight KIKBAK would
be blah-blahing on it's public blah if it didn' blah
blah in full. We've decided to go public! INSTRUCTIONS
RE RECOGNITION AND EJECTION OF PUNTERS WHO TRY TO USE
THE STAFF LIFT. (1) Keep a sharp eye posted for Mr

Amiability, himself.

With a heavy dose of smiling, he'll praise you till your nose bleeds. (2) he'll try'nd inveigle you into some phony lipping about anything -usually some crap about th the weather or sudden rise in fatstock shares. Stolidly ignore such overtures. (3) Should the punter have the gall to actually enter the lift, you should immndiately vacate it and go outside to check the sky is still there check this very carefully - take your time about it (4) If this doesn't signal to the punter that his presence is unwelcome, hahg the 'Lift Out of Order' plate up and retire to cubby-hole for a puff. (5) A problem that sometimes occurs is the 'multi-mix' when a the punter seeks to enter with an intake of legitimate staff persons. Since punters are chronic fidgeters, it might be possible to pin a button-tampering charge on them,or,failing this, to suggest that they are overweight or have B.O. (6) The hoistman should seek to be as diplomatic as possible, since punters can be verye nifty with the old shoe leather if they think they've been insulted.

\*\*\*\*\*\*\*\*\*\*\*\*\*\*\*\*\*\*\*\*\*\*\*\*\*\*\*\*\*\*\*\*\*\*\*\*\*\*\*\*\*\*\*\*\*\*\*\*\*\*\*\*\*\*

# Little
# Caesar
# Takes
# the Fall

Charlie Hazelworth had been on the door of the Centaur Social Club a hellish long time; definitely too long, claimed those disgruntled members who'd had their entry to the club baulked – often on the flimsiest of pretexts – by the feisty old Keeper of the Threshold.

Given that he was pushing seventy, he didn't pack much in the way of bounce these days – a fact he was conceited enough to ignore except when, having a bath, he was forced to confront the reality of his collapsed chest and the bleak signals of mortality emanating from his decaying kneecaps. But, like old guys the world over, Charlie H. liked to believe he could still put himself around some.

Charlie H. seemed unperturbed by the animosity his so-called 'finicky' application of the club Rules aroused. On the contrary, he treated such criticism with the contempt he judged it deserved.

'Show me a man without an enemy and I'll show you a double-dyed appeaser!' was his glib rejoinder to carping club members. Charlie H. had an abundance, in fact, a surfeit of enemies, one of the most vociferous of whom was Jim Jarvis, a car-bonnet welder in Centaur's Framing Shop (or Broadmoor as it was better known, because of its militant and highly sensitive workforce). Jarvis had been denied entry to the club by Charlie H. on the grounds that his wife 'looked suspicious'. Incensed by this blatant insult, Jarvis, not a man noted for sweetness of temper, had decked Charlie H. – a hasty overreaction, admittedly, but one, given the circumstances, that the bulk of the membership deemed totally justifiable. Despite this consensus of opinion Jarvis was given a six-months' suspension from all social-club activities.

As more complaints re Charlie H.'s growing eccentric behaviour were brought to the Committee's notice – his latest piece of mischief had been his attempt to ban the group hired for the club's annual dance because not one of them could produce a membership card – it was generally agreed, but by no means unanimously, that something would have to be done about'm. A doorman with dementia wasn't good for business. Some of the Committee, though, made light of Charlie H.'s idiosyncracies. After all, he'd proved over many years to've been a loyal and willing servant to the Club. It was, and still remained, the dominant interest of his life. To give'm the chop would be like handing'm down a death sentence – the old codger would simply go to pieces. A decision on the future of Charlie H. was, therefore, left in abeyance. However, warned president Jack Silvers, should the door-minder's future behaviour bring the Club into disrepute they'd have no option – he'd be for the bullet.

So, Charlie H. continued his now somewhat shaky reign on his cushioned chair behind the well-polished table in the club's foyer; a smallish table it was, with barely enough room to accommodate the visitors' book with ballpoint pen secured by a length of cord; the money box used for the twenty-pence fee club-visitors had to fork out; and neat piles of pontoon tickets. There was just enough room left for Charlie H.'s elbows.

And so, Charlie H. continued his truly pathetic impersonation of Edward G. Robinson as screen gangster, speech rattling from his mouth like Tommy-gun ammo, his lips bunching in what he deluded himself to be an incredible facsimile of Edward G.'s smirky grin. Charlie H.'s uncanny resemblance to the movie star had been much remarked upon – well, mentioned in passing by at least two folk: Charlie H. himself, and Sid Gattens, a guy who worked wicker to a frazzle in search of the ideal basket up at the Institute for the Blind. Charlie H. doing his Edward G. number was a riot. There's no doubt that Little Caesar would've risked crossing a dozen cop-lousy states just to shake'm by the throat!

After this near-dismissal from his portal guardian-ship, Charlie H. had become noticeably more liberal in his interpretation of the social club's Rules. It would be fair to say that since his nose's encounter with Jarvis's knuckles he'd lost not only a quart or so of his antique blood but also a considerable amount of his former zest. His doc warned'm that his heart was starting to get less'n less enthusiastic about wheeling his blood around his withering body, and renewed his urgings for Charlie H. to chuck his door job, and to settle down to a stressless retirement. But Charlie H. had scoffed at this suggestion: the image of Little Caesar in slippers or of'm Zimmering around in some Sunset Home, shitting and eating on some bureaucrat's say-so, was just too ludicrous to envisage.

One evening, though, when Charlie H. was at his post, Nemesis, in the shape of a young blonde woman, emerged from a Nightdusk Blue Super Salamander. Before closing the hatchback's passenger door, she leaned into the car and spoke briefly to its driver. He consulted his wristwatch then nodded. The blonde, who carried a red clutch-bag, snapped shut the door then, drawing her full-length black velvet cloak more tightly about'r curvaceous body, she began to thread'r way through the ranks of parked cars to the Club's entrance.

A morose-looking Charlie H., unaware as yet of the blonde's fateful approach, sat at his table in an otherwise empty foyer: apart from the pool players in the games room, most of the club members and their guests were foregathered in the main hall, where a Bingo session was underway. Thus far it'd proved to be a frustrating evening for Charlie H.: not one rule violator had turned up. He'd pinned his hopes on delivering a few knock-backs to Spunky Madden's stag-party on the often-waived Rule 4 (para 3) that debarred members from bringing more than four guests into the club at any one time – a rule that was usually gotten around by having guestless members sign them in. He'd hoped that a whispering campaign, started by Charlie H. himself, claiming that Spunky's pals were a notoriously rowdy lot, would deter club members from risking their cards through the possible misbehaviour of their sponsored guests. Spunky Madden had scuppered Charlie H.'s gambit by turning up with a multi-pass permit which, endorsed by club president, Jack Silvers, himself, also waived the visitors' fee!

'Forty-two – Little Caesar looks blue!'

And so he did. But, quite suddenly, Charlie H. felt his old brio returning. It was as if, down there in the gloomy basement of his soul, several arc-lamps had simultaneously sprung on and filled it to the brim with light.

The reason behind this mood-switch was due to the startling entrance of a very striking-looking young lady. Now, here was a female whom Charlie H., with some justification and without the attendant risk of having his nose reshaped, could've claimed looked 'suspicious'.

As the door bumped closed behind her she pushed back the hood of'r velvet cloak and her lustrous ash-blonde hair spilled onto'r shoulders. Smiling, she approached, swinging her hips, and stepping so sexily in those red stiletto-heeled shoes of hers, she could've been walking down a fashion-house catwalk instead of the grubby parquet floor-tiles of a social club.

The tap-tapping noise from her shameless shoes

ceased as she halted before the doorman's table. Charlie H. sat in the flamboyant style Little Caesar was wont to adopt when he'd 'got the world on a string', namely, tipping back his chair onto its hind legs, and rocking nice'nd easy with a big sassy grin on his chops.

'Well, Miss,' he asked the blonde, 'what can I do for you?'

After she'd told'm he sagely shook his head.

'Mr Madden's stag-party, eh?' He allowed the chair legs to settle on the floor, then planted his elbows on the table. Slowly, he shook his head. 'Now I know these old peepers of mine aren't much good for anything these days, but believe me, Miss, they're still good enough to tell me that there's nothing "staggish" about you – not from where I'm sitting, anyway.'

'Cut the crap, Gramps!' she snapped. 'I'm running late as it is.'

Although the 'Gramps' crack was a real ego-melter, Little Caesar was too wily a poker player to let so much as a flicker of annoyance ruffle his brow. He nodded. 'Okay, supposing you tell me what your business with Mr Madden is about?' He raised an appeasing hand, which probably saved'm from being on the receiving end of yet another waspish remark. Nevertheless, the blonde glowered at'm.

'Who are you, Miss? What d'you want?'

She looked startled, maybe even unnerved by his snappish 'Don't-mess-with-me-I'm-Edward-G.!' snarl, which when accompanied by his Little Caesar scowl was truly devastating. Yep, he was in charge once more.

'Well?'

74

She told'm.

'You're a what?'

'You heard, Mister.'

Charlie took some time to get his face together again, but he somehow managed. He grinned up at'r. 'Lady,' he chortled, 'if you're a Singing Telegram then I'm a whistling kettle!'

Placing her red clutchbag on the table, the blonde began to undo the belt of her sombre cloak. 'Okay, Gramps, if it's proof you want – how's this?' Dramatically, she flung her cloak wide, giving the goggle-eyed Charlie H. a close-up of her tarty undies: these consisted of a scarlet, lightly-boned lace basque with black silk trimmings, a pair of skimpy black satin briefs; tautly-suspendered fishnet stockings, and, of course, the red ultra high-heeled shoes.

'My working gear, right? Just give's the nod when you've had your fill.' The impact her erotic pose was having upon Charlie H. was incalculable, although certain giveaway signs were evident, for instance his Adam's apple bobbing frantically, a tremble travelling the length of his limbs, and a flickering sensation that tickled across his thighs. With'r blatantly provocative display, the blonde was revealing, not only her lingerie but also her abysmal ignorance re the frailty of old men's vital organs, and, no less crucial, the damage that can be wreaked upon a septuagenarian's libido when, as now, it's shaken so roughly from its sexual coma. As disorientated as an old crow clinging to a storm-spun weathervane, Charlie H. could feel his blood fluttering at his wrists, his throat, and at all points within its compass.

Recalling the blonde Jezebel's instruction, Charlie H. weakly nodded: the peepshow was over; the 'curtains' closed in a silent collision of black velvet.

Moments later, Jack Boag, the trim shop inspector, entered the foyer from the main hall. 'You the telegram thingy?' he asked looking the girl up'n down.

She nodded.

'You're late.' He grinned lasciviously. 'But don't worry – most of'm are still on their feet. C'mon.' He made a hand gesture. 'I'll show you where it's at.'

Pausing only to uplift'r clutchbag, the girl came clip-clopping around the doorman's table and crossed to join Boag, who was keeping the door ajar by propping the sole of his shoe against it.

'You okay, then, Charlie?' he called out, arousing 'Shurrups' from those nervy Bingoites who were waiting on one for the 'Snowball'. From Charlie H., himself, he got a mournful little lift of the shoulders that was followed by a deep, shuddering sigh.

Door squealing open.

Girl's voice saying something about 'a dirty old man . . .'

Boag laughing: 'C'mon, old Charlie doesn't even know he's got one these days' . . . Door squealing shut.

A long silence broken by someone shouting:

'Forty-four! Who's on the door?'

'Wee Charlie!' they roar.

But it was a false call. By then Charlie H. was standing in a long, winding queue. The man next to'm said: 'I hear tell this St Peter bloke's helluva pick'n choosy about who he lets in.'

Charlie H. nodded his approval. But all the way to the Gates the same worry nagged at him. 'Wouldn't Little Caesar look just a touch ridiculous wearing wings?'

## CENTAUR STAFF DANCE FIASCO.

The annual Centaur Staff Dance wasn't the success that'd
been expected. A fist fight on the dance floor during
the aptly named 'Pandamonium Tango' set the tone for the
evening. The fisticuffs were between Bertrand de Witz
and Mabel Klondyke, the latter claiming that de Witz,
while executing an extravagant dance step had dented her
pram. De Witz had added insult to injury by claiming
that a dance floor was no place to be walking a
chimpanzee, in any case.Taking exception to his remark,
the babe clocked de Witz with its feeding bottle then
made off with a mad series of screeches and chattering
De Witz, while in hot pursuit of the nappified litle
terror was unfortunately cut down by an articulated
lorry that had most surprisingly come charging from
behind a  ruck of St Bernards Waltzers.

The undoubted highlight of this low key evening
was the alluring routine of Balaclva-Stripper,Miss
Trudy Twickelpoons Lit only by wavering candles and
tightly surrounded by slavering men, Trudy seductively
peeled off at least 70 balaclavas, stripping to her
bare head, although, to maintain public decency, she
wore an eye patch.

The dance ended with the singing of "Should old
Acquaintance Be Forgot?" to which the unanimous
responce was "Yes - Definitely!"

The revelers left in a fleet of especially layed-on
black buses, which this year, as a safety precaution
had Bars in all of their windows and two policemen
acting as escorts in each vehichle.

# PRIME MINISTER NOT TO OPEN LOCKER

Britain's Prime Minister has graciously agreed not
to open the new state-of-the-art Locker (Model E/231)
which was the surprise hit of the Kirkcudbright Trades
Fair Exhibition.

Said the Premier " Frankly, I couldn't miss the
opportunity nøt to open this fantastic loøker which
represents (insert numerous "blah--blahs here)
...The locker's special feature is it's revolutionary
cutaway tungsten steel peg which will "be a great help
on rainy days," commented love-in lockermates John and
Simon, as they fussed.over draperies and scattered
cushions with pkayful abandon. " Really," sighed Simon,
"it's like a nightmare-come-truue. Especially having
someone as unimportant  as the P.M. not coming to open
our Joe Cocker....

SAD FOOTNOTE
Papa Westray, Centaur's most northerly alcoholic, died
shortly after " opening time" during the op to have
his cones hoisted and gale stones removed.  Burial at
sea.  No teetota llers,please.

# Boag's
# Gallery

Interrupted at prayer in the foremen's locker room, Alf
Sheridan, down on one knee, hastily pretended to be
tying his shoelaces. He glanced up at the blue-suited
Stan Cutter as he approached from the far end of the
locker file, ' 'To Stan,' said the greyback, rising,
'what're you doing on the bat-shift?' Apparently,
Cutter had shift-swopped with Gus Levin to allow'm
to play a bowling tie.

Sheridan nodded. 'Right, Stan, what's your problem.' When Cutter, the Senior Sequencer, came
looking for you, there just had to be a problem: tonight
proved no exception. As soon as the nightshift got
underway, Cutter wanted to sub a rogue body on the
trim-line. Sheridan jotted down the shell's sequence/
chassis numbers, then noted details of the sub. Pro-
ducing a cigarette, Cutter tapped it a couple of times

on the back of his skinny hand. 'Oh, and another thing,' he said as he dipped the cig into his lighter's flame, 'the loading bay hoist-crane's knackered again. Chain's bust.' Sheridan nodded, then took a roll of sticky tape from his locker and, stooping, began to patch a rip in the bulky black plastic bag at his feet.

Cutter, inhaling smoke in stressful little bursts, watched for a time, then his gaze wandered to the photograph Sheridan had taped to the inner side of his locker door. It was of a girl with a comet of red hair who wore a university graduation gown and was posed seated with a boxed scroll in her long, pale hands. Her eyes were the exact shade of the new colour Centaur had introduced that very week – Mermaid Green. Cutter nodded at the picture. 'Your daughter, right?'

Sheridan, his rough surgery on the plastic bag completed, rose and lobbed the tape roll onto his locker shelf. He nodded. 'That's my Joyce. She's lecturing in London now. Doing very well.'

'Mine does all her lecturing at home,' Cutter said. He took a withering draw on the cig then, with a smoky sigh, murmured, 'Well, back to the treadmill, I suppose.'

When Cutter's footsteps had faded, Sheridan took a well-thumbed bible from his locker and let it fall open at random. His gaze settled on the first verse it encountered. 'Be sober, be vigilant,' he read, 'because your adversary, the devil, as a roaring lion, walketh about seeking whom he may devour.'

There was a major event that night – The Widow was sabotaged! A person or persons had gone into the transfer tunnel and lashed a laden, outgoing sling to an empty returner with a steel hawser. As a result, when The Widow started up, yards of tracking had been wrenched from roof supports, and three car-shells, maybe even four, were said to be on the deck.

Zombieland was in uproar. The Panic-Wagon, its acid-orange lamps flashing, had gone wailing to the breakdown scene. Harried-looking tradesmen along with their tool-burdened mates ran in the same direction. A sarcastic rumour was going the rounds that a spanner-wrestler and a spark had already keeled over'n died, their systems unable to withstand the shock of being confronted by a major crisis in the shift's first hour – a period which traditionally involved tea-swigging and practice at unassisted walking.

Apart from the sporadic clatterings of trucking movements – the paint hospital was still disgorging shells – things were quiet in the trim shop: operators basked in the silence of the sabotaged Widow. They stood chatting along the walls or played cards and slurped tea at smoke-hazed tables. Fast-winged rumours, taking off from their gossip-hives, buzzed far and wide, tickling the ears of the credulous with fantastic lies: The Widow's back was broken; it'd take days if not weeks to fix it; they were all on the verge of being Sent Up The Road; the Big Wheel, himself, George C. Warrender, was said to've left Stateside in his private plane, accompanied by the infamous Detroit Gate-Slammers Squad which had only a shave and a shirt-change ago returned from a 'lock'm and leave'm' mission to Centaur's Middle-East kit-plant operation.

Ops like the vinyl-roofers and the sill-fixers

remained on the job, while some other men chose to work beyond their stations so they could enjoy the break later when the Widow started up.

A couple of greybacks gossiped at the top of the estate storage line and through the building there was the usual drift of traffic: Gil Peters ferrying drums of underseal from the paint-storage area; a citron and black striped garbage truck droning between bin areas; a fire-bug zipping across the storage apron, its driver, Tommy Derwent, casting suspicious glances about himself, as if everyone he encountered was a potential arsonist.

Sheridan took advantage of the stoppage by getting the trim-line snagger and the spare man to work-up the insert body requested by Cutter. Leaving them to this he went out onto the loading bay to check the knackered hoist. A dayshift fitter'd been at work on it for its heavy chain lay coiled on the concrete floor and some of the hoist's parts were spread on a piece of sacking. Sheridan reckoned there'd be no need to lift any shells in from the storage yard tonight, especially now that a lengthy major line stoppage was underway, but to be on the safe side, Sheridan decided to report the fault again.

From the inspection booth, an aluminium structure which sat athwart the underseal ramp, Jack Boag bayed Sheridan's name. The greyback paused. Why'd Boag always have to play to the gallery? Did he think he was deaf? Roaring like that, focusing the attention of those gawkers lined along the wall with nothing weightier on their minds than smoking and gossip. Boag emerged from the booth and came across the grid. His red hair had a foxy coarseness to it and was plentiful enough to afford a pair of extravagantly long sidelocks and an arrowhead beard. Before he reached Sheridan, who stood waiting below the grid rail, Boag lobbed a set of car keys at'm which the greyback had to look lively to catch.

'What's the verdict, then?'

Boag laid his tattooed arms along the rail. 'It might make it to the nearest scrappy.' He waited until Sheridan's face had wearied of its forced smile before he continued: 'Know what, Alf? I reckon that daughter of yours should be had up for cruelty to gearboxes. And you, too, for aiding and abetting her.' The greyback's fixed smile was forced into an encore. 'Never seen such a trashed-up box. Letting her loose on an ace machine like that! Boag shook his head. 'Criminal, that was, Alf. I mean you don't learn the fiddle practising on a Strad, do you?'

Sheridan nodded, conceding the point.

'Gear selectors badly worn and replaced. Same with camshaft. Same track rod ends. Same cylinder head gasket. Couldn't source the sporadic knocking sound you were on about – maybe the car practising its death-rattle when Joyce got behind the wheel. The suspension was a bit on the flabby side and –'

Sheridan held his hand aloft in a silencing gesture. 'Fine, Jack. Get it all down on paper and I'll see to it. Okay?'

Boag stretched and yawned. 'Only fair to warn you, Alf – the bill's gonna be a bitch.'

Sheridan dropped the car keys into his overall pocket. 'Just so long as it gets by its MOT.' His neck was beginning to cramp, and being forced to stare up at the op wasn't doing a lot for his psychological stance either.

'Legit comes expensive, Alf. Specially when the job calls for loadsa heavy spannering. Beats me why you didn't shop more local like.' Boag winked. 'Y'know, called up your friendly Magpie Service –'

'Robbing one's employer is despicable!'

'Amen, to that, brother!' said Boag, giving him a mock salute before turning to pad back to his aluminium cage. As he did so, he was sarcastically bawling one of Sheridan's favourite hymns: 'Onward Christian soldiers . . .'

Slipping from the building via a side door Sheridan crossed to the battered-looking hut which stood adjacent to the water-storage tank. Its water level was high and turbulent, so much so that freshets continually splashed over the tank's rim. The hut door squealed as Sheridan pushed it ajar, not too widely but just enough to allow'm to poke his head into the dark interior. He heard what he'd expected to hear, namely, a drunkard's shameless and reverberating snores. With the tails of his coat overall flying, he recrossed the yard. The hut's occupant was Hugh Kelsey, of course. Sheridan had been aware of the deception right from the start. The men for their part were well aware that their greyback turned a blind eye to Kelsey's frequent absences from the masking grid, that he feigned not to notice that they took it in turns to sacrifice their own breaks. To a man the squad was involved in a conspiracy of kindness, the aim of which was the slender hope that Kelsey might emerge from his private Hell where the flame of alcohol seemed intent on expunging his life just as pitilesssly as fire had devoured his entire family. Not for a minute did Sheridan share his squad's optimism that Kelsey's grief might somehow burn itself out, but for the time being, at least, he continued with the charade. After all, the situation presented him with the bonus of the men's cooperation when, occasionally, he asked them to work beyond the bounds of their man-assignments. Furthermore, by going along with the deception, he retained the squad's respect – something not to be sniffed at in the Centaur Car Plant, whose outrageous slag-rag, KIKBAK, in a recent issue had seen fit to define a greyback as 'a patch of industrial fog, usually to be found lurking in corners but seldom seen in working areas'.

Back at his desk at the top of the trim-line, Sheridan entered a couple of memos in the section diary: these concerned the loading-bay hoist and a complaint from a shoppy regarding puddles from roof leaks affecting the working area – a possible safety hazard. With the memos completed, Sheridan capped his pen and returned it to his pocket. The Widow's repairs seemed likely to last a longish time yet, so he'd have to keep tabs on the empty trolley supply to the paint shop. He flicked backwards through the diary pages, finding a sorry record of lost production, most of which was down to line-dispute stoppages. This business tonight, what had the saboteur or saboteurs hoped to gain by it in the long run? Madness, it was, sheer lunacy. Last week, for instance, there'd been the devilish work of some maniac who'd strolled down a line of Sultans dragging a file or some such tool along their paintwork – damage amounting to thousands of pounds. And for what? To hit back at the System. Was that it? You wounded your enemy by cutting your own throat!

Sheridan paused at a diary entry he'd made – it seemed a lifetime ago – concerning a minor line stoppage due to a sling circulator fault. But the entry remained unfinished. Sheridan's jaw tightened: Death had intervened here, had crept up behind him in the guise of Ted Bullock, who told'm that there'd been a phone call, that he must go home at once. And that had been how his familiar domestic existence had ended, the amputation of an optimism that his marriage would go on untroubled for many a year to come.

He gazed at the static lines of car bodies. In a way his own life was like that now, immobilised, out-of-action. It too had been sabotaged. What made it worse was that Joyce, his daughter, had played a prime role in this wrecking of his future hopes. She'd chucked her academic career, tossed it aside, as if all those years of study and sacrifice meant nothing to her. 'She's lecturing in London now.' What a stupid lie! He should've come straight out with the truth: 'Joyce? Oh, haven't you heard? She's into modelling now. Yes, abandoned her academic career. Too boring, she says. Well, that's modern youth for you. Always craving novelty. And there's me getting my hopes raised that maybe, just maybe, she'd apply for a professional appointment closer to home.'

'But, Dad, you can't expect me to throw up everything to come back here . . . I'm sorry, it just isn't possible.' Joyce's words returned to him from the vault of that awesome day. Of course it hadn't been possible. Not really. Fashion models had to be able to fly off at a moment's notice. The baggage of an ageing parent was the last thing such mobile and talented people could afford. Besides, as she'd mentioned before, her agent had strong hopes of getting her into the Paris fashion circuit. Wasn't that exciting? Yes, my darling daughter, I can't think of anything more exciting. Sorry? Could I teach you to – what? To drive? Well, that depends, doesn't it, on how long you plan to stay. A fortnight to three weeks, eh? Time enough to show you the rudiments, that's about all . . .

Joyce had, in fact, extended her stay to just over two months, then she'd made her departure, leaving Sheridan with a broken heart and a wrecked gearbox, not to mention, from some dark area of his mind, a late, unwanted gift for irony.

A movement by his side interrupted his musings. Maurice Henshaw, Boag's partner in the inspection booth, stood there. As usual he looked hopelessly lost inside his overlarge boilersuit, an industrial waif with specs that magnified the timidity of his gaze. When he spoke his dentures clacked, and he always seemed to have a boil plaster stuck to his plooky face. A new-start in the trim shop, word had got around that he was a scoutmaster, and with cruel inevitability he'd been nicknamed Woggle.

'Ah, Maurice,' Sheridan said, 'I was just on my way to see you.' From beneath his desk he dragged out the plastic bag. 'Here's the stuff I promised for your jumble sale.' He placed the bag at Henshaw's feet. 'It's mostly my late wife's things, coats, hats, dresses, and so on. Some shoes, too – hardly been worn.'

Henshaw thanked him, but his tone sounded lifeless, uninterested. Something else on his mind, had he? A jumpy sort of look to'm, not that this meant much – the man was a bag of nerves at the best of times. He seemed to be on the brink of broaching something. With murky fingernails he plucked at the boil plaster, threatening to reveal its underlying corruption. Maybe he'd embarrassed the poor devil by presenting him with the jumble-sale stuff in full view of the squad. Hardly likely, for, judging by the racket they were making over their card game, they weren't in the least interested in what went on around them. Sheridan indicated the bag. 'You can pick this up later if you like.'

'No, I'll take it now.'

His fingernails were still tampering with the boil plaster.

'You all right, Maurice? Not sick or anything?'

Henshaw shook his head, then, with a startling blush, he stammered a question. Sheridan turned the query over in his mind, seeking out the reason for it. 'But why d'you want a move? I thought you were doing all right in the booth.'

'I am – I was.'

'Well, then?'

Henshaw's flush deepened. 'I'd rather not say.'

Sheridan studied him. 'It's not Boag, is it? I know he can be a bit of a wag.'

Henshaw bent to take a grip on the bag.

'Wait,' said Sheridan, 'let's talk about this.'

Plucking his pen from his overall pocket the grey-back tapped it on his desk. 'You want a move, right?' Henshaw nodded. 'Well, maybe I can arrange that. But I have to know why. So, let's have it.'

Viperlike, Henshaw's tongue darted out to moisten his lips. He took a deep breath then blurted: 'It's those filthy photos! Everywhere you turn. I can't stand'm.'

So, that was it – Boag's Gallery, a disgusting collection of pin-ups, the lewd and nauseous cullings from porn mags and tabloid Page 3s with which Boag had chosen to besmirch the walls of the inspection booth. Similar erotic muck could be seen plant-wide, and though Sheridan considered the booth's display to be not only offensive, but utterly depraved, his fellow greybacks seemed to think they were harmless enough.

Henshaw's dentures continued their desolate clacking. 'It's not just the pictures, it's all those perverts who come to swap tapes and magazines – sometimes you can't get moving for them.'

Sheridan nodded but said nothing. He recognised that a dangerous moment was presenting itself; a time for caution, for diplomacy. 'Custom and practice' was a key phrase for the Centaur worker. It was a reef plainly visible to those whose job it was to negotiate the warping undercurrents of factory politics, an area littered with the wreckage of innovators and 'Do-it-my-way!' whizz-kids. Boag's Gallery had been in the inspection booth a long time, so long in fact that it had practically become a shop-floor institution; operators from as far away as the press shop, or from the rectification area in MAD, came to ogle its vileness. The Gallery had become the industrial equivalent of a red-light district and the wily Boag exploited the lecherous tourist trade by making the charge of admission to his peepshow one porny magazine or a sexy picture of exceptional crudity. By this ploy Boag's Gallery increased daily both in size and corruptness, spreading itself like a malignant tumour. To storm Boag's filth-hole, to lay the biting lash of his righteous wrath on the flesh of those wall-browsing degenerates, had long been Sheridan's ambition, but when it'd come to enacting it he'd always – what was the prevalent idiom for cowardice again? Bottled? Yes, he'd always bottled it. The Bull wouldn't've hesitated – by now he'd've had a squad of ops in the booth, stripping off Boag's erotic wallpaper. Henshaw's tongue flickered forth to dab spittle along his parched lips. Sherman frowned. Why'd he keep doing that? Gave you the shudders. Like talking to a blasted snake.

'Have you spoken to Boag about this?' he asked.

Henshaw's drooping shoulders twitched. 'I get enough stick as it is.'

'But you're willing to make an official complaint?'

Henshaw bent to lift the plastic bag.

'You see,' the greyback explained, 'my hands're tied –'

'Forget it, then!'

Sheridan was surprised by the operator's waspish tone. 'I just thought . . .'

'What?'

Henshaw stood there with the crackling bag in his arms. How pathetically gawky he looked, a complete pushover. The boil he'd been tampering with had finally burst: from under the plaster's soiled and ruffled lower edge pus had begun to ooze. Henshaw shook his head in a slow, resigned fashion.

'Something should be done – it just isn't right . . .'

Damn! there he goes with that reptile stuff again. Why couldn't he keep his beastly tongue in his mouth where it belonged?

'Leave it with me,' Sheridan said. 'I'll see what I can do.' The round-shouldered Henshaw gave'm a surly nod, said something the foreman was unable to make out, then carried off the bag of shoes and clothing. A shudder passed through Sheridan's body. Maybe it'd something to do with the hobgoblinish look of the man, but the odd fancy of Satan making off with a bag of freshly-caught souls troubled'm.

Sheridan was already regretting his rash promise. Something lacking brakes had been nudged into motion, something that would gather more and more speed as it found its true downward and irresistible course.

An hour had passed and The Widow still remained motionless. It could be likened to an industrial coronary, the Centaur stricken, down on its knees. Having ensured that the paint shop had a plentiful supply of trolleys, Sheridan chased up the hoist-repair job again. But soon he could put it off no longer – the business with Boag.

Stan Cutter, who'd gone through to Broadmoor to assist one of his squad with a sequence change, had during his absence given Sheridan the use of his office. The greyback sat there now behind a table cluttered with specification tallies and model plates. Also on the table was a small tranny with its back removed to expose its Japanese innards. Obviously, Cutter'd been fiddling with it for nearby lay a screwdriver, a soldering iron, and a loop of solder. Sheridan stared intently at the radio's workings, looking in vain for the fault, the loose connection.

He gave a sigh and pushed the tranny aside. In a way the Boag problem was proving to be equally intractable. There'd be no profit in reading the riot act to'm, nor even in cutting up rough. Equally pointless would be a diatribe against the evils of pornography. The man was totally addicted to lewd voyeurism. Away back when he and Boag had been neighbours, he'd learned of his unsavoury tastes. Sheridan's wife, Marjory, had predicted that the lecher would be consumed in a Hellfire fuelled by his smutty and depraved magazines. The image of Boag yelping and shrieking at the fiery heart of an ever-burning, unquenchable inferno of pin-up mags always had an irresistibly tonic effect on Sheridan. But not this time; a downmouth mood had'm in its jaws. He glanced at his wristwatch then, taking up the screwdriver, he began to drum its blade on the tabletop. It was typical of Boag to make'm wait, especially since he'd stressed to Logan, the squad's shoppy, that he wanted to see'm at once.

Sheridan stopped fiddling with the screwdriver and placed it firmly back on the table. Why so jumpy? They were going to have a straight man-to-man talk, that was all. Nothing drastic, nothing too heated. No, what he intended to use was a gambit, one that maybe bore a pinch too much compromise, a ducking of the real issue. A little clot of shame slid through him as he remembered the incident in the locker-room when

Cutter had come barging in on his prayer. Was he about to 'tie his shoelaces' again?

Floating up the passageway between the storage lines, his head and shoulders visible above the shiny Sunburst Red roofs of car-shells, came Boag. He'd hitched a ride on Tommy Derwent's firebug, one of the battery-driven runarounds used by the plant firemen to ferry them, according to the joke, from one burning mug of char to the next. Sheridan watched as the firebug emerged from a ruck of flame-red Salamanders, and then turned in the direction of Cutter's office. To his intense annoyance, Sheridan again found himself drumming on the table with the screwdriver blade.

Boag must've mouthed some kind of quip to Derwent, for the latter's grin made his yellowish face look for a moment like a gashed melon. His passenger dropped lightly from the firebug then came storming into the office. By hooking a baseball-booted foot under its spar he dragged a chair towards himself then promptly slapped himself down on it. One leg now rose to straddle the other. In body language he was plainly saying: 'Right, jerk, lay out your stuff – the meter's running!' With the usual sardonic smirk scribbled across his lips, he tilted the chair onto its creaking back legs. But as Sheridan began to mouth his rehearsed opening gambit it was immediately made plain to'm that he wasn't going to get the op's undivided attention, for Boag, spotting the tranny on the cluttered table, immediately took it in hand and began to examine it. Next, he pointed to the screwdriver: 'Gimme dat ting – why doncha!' Boag demanded in that parodic gangster voice he sometimes affected. Leaning across the table, he snatched the tool from the startled foreman's grasp.

Boag's shrewd gaze raked the tranny, then with the screwdriver blade he began to probe various locations on the printed circuit board. Sheridan had begun to feel like a tranny himself, one that'd been left yawking unheard in a corner. The greyback paused to check out what kind of impact he was registering on the smirking devil – a big fat zero by the look of it. Boag continued to poke with the screwdriver. Sheridan would even have settled for the half-cocked eyebrow which usually accompanied the op's sarcastic quips, any clue at all which indicated that he was being listened to and not merely recycling words. Boag rose and, taking up the soldering iron, plugged it into a wall socket. The greyback tried to check his annoyance at the other's studied indifference but soon this was no longer sustainable: his exasperation boiled to the surface. 'Am I talking to myself, or what?'

Boag balanced the iron on the table's edge. 'I'm hearing you loud'n clear, Alf.'

'Well?'

'Seems, if I've got this right, that should a virgin from the sewing room – eye the sky for winged bacon, folks! – get transferred to the booth I've to take down her nix, sorry, I've to take down my pix.' Again that insolent smirk. 'You're absolutely spot-on, Alf. It could shock'r cold, suddenly finding herself surrounded by all them tits and slits.'

'Must you be so crude!'

'Y'now me, Alf, never call a tit a mammary-gland if I can help it.'

'You'll do it, then?'

Boag checked out the soldering iron by spitting on its warming tip. Evidently it wasn't hot enough yet for he replaced it on the table's edge.

'I was hoping we might've worked something out amicably,' Sheridan said.

Testing the iron again – this time his spittle fairly sizzled on its heated tip – Boag positioned it above the transistor's entrails. 'You don't have the right to ask,' he said as he homed in on the loose connection. 'There I am,' he went on, 'stuck'n that fuck'n biscuit tin for hours on end. Try it sometime. Never a minute. You've to send for a snagger if you want to scratch your arse. So, I stick a few birds up and –'

'A few thousand, you mean!'

'So what?'

A globule of solder dropped exactly where required. 'There, that's got it!' He turned over the tranny and pressed a button: there was an immediate outburst of music. Boag switched it off, then screwed on the cover. As he unplugged the soldering iron Sheridan said to him: 'They're coming down, Jack, whether you like it or not.'

'As the hooker said to the sailor!' Boag jabbed the hot iron into the sand in the fire-bucket. He sauntered back to the table. It creaked as he leaned his weight on it. 'Alf,' he said, 'you're doing it again – letting that rag on your back fool you.'

'I don't see what –'

'And such a Holy Joe with it.' Boag raised a hand.

'Don't say a word, Alf, not one bloody lip-squeak, or I might just get tempted to tell you something that'd blow that halo of yours into orbit.' Boag went to the door but as he opened it, he paused to say over his shoulder, 'They're staying put, Alf, every last one. And you can tell that fuck'n monk-in-a-boilersuit Woggle I said so!'

The door shut with a jarring crash.

Vic Logan, the underseal shoppy, shook his head in disbelief. 'I don't get it,' he said. 'You saying for a bunch of tit-fodder you'd risk a –'

'A what?' Sheridan demanded. 'A walk-off? Credit the punters with some sense.'

The discussion was in progress at Sheridan's desk. Logan, who'd at first been treating the matter as a joke, began to look more serious. 'What's with a few pin-ups, anyway?' he asked. 'They're all over the place.'

'I want that muck off the booth walls by tonight.'

'You're having me on!'

Sheridan sensed that he was pushing too hard. Stupid, setting a time-limit. Losing the place. The nonsense was gathering momentum. Boag's remarks had upset'm, no doubt about that, but he still held the initiative. How many punters would support Boag when the chips were down? They'd become the laughing-stock of the plant. Imagine going home to tell your wife you were on strike over a bunch of tatty porn!

Logan must've been thinking along similar lines. He said: 'Tell you what: if'nd when a female comes to work in the booth, I'll call a meeting and put what you're after to the lads. Okay?'

It was time, Sheridan decided, to get off the hook. A face-saving exercise was called for. But sooner than later he'd wangle a female inspector into the booth. He was on the point of accepting Logan's proposal when a burst of laughter and hand-clapping twitched his glance to the underseal ramp. The men were cheering a grotesque figure, a travesty got up in a floral dress, a beige felt hat, his overlarge feet half-crushed into ladies' shoes. It was Boag! Hands on hips, he tottered to and fro on an improvised catwalk made from a strip of cardboard laid on the underseal grid. To continued claps, shouts, and whistles of encouragement, Boag gyrated his hips, then began to perform a mock striptease, lewdly raising the dress to show his rolled-up overalls beneath it. Every cell in Sheridan's body seemed to vibrate with rage. The dress Boag was so obscenely flaunting had been the very one his wife Marjory'd worn to Joyce's graduation ceremony. The hat – it flew from Boag's head as he performed a rumbustious can-can – was the one she'd often worn to church.

'Make'm stop!' Sheridan hissed through clenched teeth.

'It's only a bit of fun.' Logan was as amused as the rest of the squad. His smile quickly vanished though when Sheridan leaned towards him and said viciously in his ear: 'You can tell Boag if he doesn't get that muck off the booth walls within the next half-hour, Kelsey's for the high-jump!'

'Kelsey?'

'That's right. I know, and you know, he's lying blitzed in the tank hut!'

The men watched in silence from their table as Boag cropped his Gallery from the booth walls. Naked ladies fell at his feet like rancid snow. Boag's face was expressionless. The rip-ripping sound went on and on. Sheridan stood on the ramp, just outside the booth's entrance. The den of iniquity was being cleansed at last. But this produced in the watching greyback no sense whatsoever of triumph or elation; how would he ever be able to rip from his mind the moment when Logan, having called the squad together, announced to them Sheridan's ultimatum? It would remain there, clinging obscenely, that collective glower the betrayed squad had fixed on him. He stood now on the edge of their contempt, his blood winding through his body like a slow poison.

The ripping sounds in the booth ceased. Boag, still expressionless, waded through the piles of salacious cuttings. How naked the booth walls looked now, shorn of their vile 'erotic wallpaper'. Boag paused to confront Sheridan. 'Saved this one for you, squire,' he said as from his pocket he produced a page from a glossy magazine and passed it to'm. Sheridan unfolded it. His eyes flinched. A naked young woman with a comet of red hair was to be seen kneeling before an equally nude man and he – Sheridan tore the page to bits, but it was already too late. What he'd seen couldn't be unseen – the repulsive image was now just one more item of grief luggage for him to tote around.

'Great thing, education, Alf,' Boag said gruffly. 'I suppose that was her taking her orals!'

From all over the trimshop there arose loud shouts as with a rapid series of jerks The Widow began to move. In the scramble of operators making their way to man their stations, Sheridan walked unnoticed across the floor and went out onto the loading bay. He crossed to where the the hoist parts lay on a piece of sacking. Bending, he began to gather up the chain, laying it in clanking loops over his arm. Bearing the weight of it, he moved towards the exit and went out into the yard.

Thirty paces would take him to the water tank.

## VERSE   AND   WERSE!

SPUNKY MADDENS STAGGY.

Now the party was applaudn'm
As he took a swig of ladunum
Then a nostrilful of 'snow'
To clear his head
Munching marijuana
He thumped that old pianna
And bawled: Lets move it,cats
This Staggy's dead!
He played'm swingy blues
As he belted back the booze,
He only stopped to fill his
Hypo syringe.
He warned: 'You'll know what
Trash is
When I start mainlining hashish
Twas enough t make the strong-
est of them cringe.
They groaned 'this guy's
depressin'
As he puffed cannabis resin,
And crunched lysergic acid
cubes galore.
But when he voted for an orgy
With a curvy chick called
Georgie
They had gently nailed'm to the
Floor.
Punters heed this warning
Lest you wake up one morning
And get the urge to give your
mind a booster.
Soon you'll see the grief you've
bought
When your brain begins th rot,
And you can't build them cars
the way you yooster !

SONG OF THE MAD FLEA.

Oh, woe is me
A little flea
That is what I'm ur.
A skinny rat is my abode
mongst its mangy fur
I hop my lousy life away
The pong is really chronic
Oh, what a destiny to be
At the seat of things bubonic
This 'world' of mine
Spends all its time
Im gorgin grub'nd swillling.
I'm humped around
Midst stinks profo nd,
Unasked, what's more –
Unwilling.
But soon, some day,
Not far away's
I'll go alone'nd forage.
 When this big greedy git is
Dead,
From eating poisoned porage!


FANGS AINT W OT THEY USED TO BE
    Don't drink me  Drac,
    The victim gasped,
    I suffered bad from asthma!
    That's quite alright
    The monster rasped,
I only want your plathsma!

## MODESTY SHIELDS FOR MALE OPS

Complaints made by male ops that their female counterparts are looking up their trouser-legs on the high
track are being investigated.Said one blushing male:
'I've never met such a shower of ankle-oglers.There's
just no level they wouldn't stoop to for a glimpse of a
hairy ham.' A female haughtily denied this claim. 'It's
bad enough having to look at the creeeps. ' At that
moment a cherubic little male op seated himself in a
nearby picnic area andcoyly crossed his ankels.
'Jeepers grab them sexy shins!' she said lecherously,
and hurried off to give'r equally shinful colleages
the war.

# The
# Poacher

In the boardroom of the Centaur Car Company the Martians were drinking coffee from plastic cups and smoking cigarettes. Between the swigs and the cigs, they said technical things like: 'We've got to up the quality' or 'We won't beat the Japs if we keep shipping gaps . . .'

With all of his managerial know-how, each member of the team was striving to look laid-back, although to a man each one of them was scared rigid that he'd miss one of the Supreme Martian's jokes. What's more, every one of them was terrified of being on the receiving end of a bollocking from him: men had been known to've walked with a limp or to've been seen talking to lampposts after an earbashing from the S.M.

But today their boss had been in an amiable mood. Harmoniously, these boardroom vets had worked their way through a hefty problems pad and were now in the process of tying up details of the final item on the agenda. It'd been a real toughie. The problem set for them had been this: how d'you build a car to unusually high standards without letting the workforce in on it?

The SM ticked off this item. 'Right,' he said, 'we run it as a Show Car. We're all agreed on that?' He addressed himself now specifically to his prod/con manager, Mal Kibbley. 'The question now is – what day, Mal?'

Made to flush by the bounty of being addressed by his forename – a rare honour for any Martian – Kibbley cleared his throat. 'The position's patchy,' he informed the group, then began to drone his way through quality performances linked to specific days and specific hours, a dialogue laced with totem phrases like 'Monday cars', 'Friday-build jobs', 'labour-force imponderables', 'response to campaign thrusts . . .' Accompanying this techno-tripe there was much jiggling with flow-charts and build-stats. Kibbley was, in fact, just getting into his verbal stride when the S.M. held up a restraining hand.

'Okay, Mal – the more you feed the donkey, the more it shits!' It was one of those salty sayings for which their boss was renowned, and his fellow Martians wasted no time in according it loud guffaws. Even Kibbley, who'd suffered a 'quantitative dip' in prestige, was, nevertheless, at pains to crank up a smile.

'We'll make it Wednesday,' declared the SM. 'I want it on track and running by 0900 hours.' He tapped the table with his pen. 'And let me stress once more – this job's to go through from Bales to Sales without so much as a scratch. Understood?'

The Martians' heads bobbed like corks on troubled waters.

Stan Cutter's job made a coronary attack not only inevitable but a future event to be savoured. Bearing the title of Senior Sequencer, it appeared that his main task was to jiggle like a purple-faced puppet on the end of telephone wires. Cutter was often to be seen bawling dementedly into his telephone, and when he really cracked up he'd been known to kick the jangling instrument around his tiny office. Today, though, things were going relatively smoothly for Cutter. As far as he knew there were only three cock-ups on track – a wrong colour; a wrong drive; and a 'roofer' minus its rack. All three errors were down to Biggles Blane, a sequencer who, according to Cutter, was a half-witted ape who'd managed to wangle his way past the gate-snipes disguised as a human. Biggles, whose nickname had been derived from the pilot's helmet he'd once sported to 'protect his brain-cell', as one wag put it, had an IQ on par with a bag of wet sawdust.

He'd begun work for Centaur in the press shop, but they'd got shot of'm after only a few weeks because they claimed he 'upset the steel'. His transfer to the body'n white section had been swiftly curtailed after he'd managed to break his greyback's heart and the clocking-on-machine, both on the same morning.

Biggles had been shunted around the plant more often than a 'holiday-eve special'. He eventually wound up in the water-test booth, where he might've quietly rusted away if a vacancy for a sequencer hadn't arisen. The thought of wearing a collar'n tie and having a jacket pocket brimming with pens had appealed to Biggles. So, to immense sighs of relief from greybacks plant-wide, Biggles ceased to be an hourly-paid op and took up the staff position of Sequencer.

Cutter's suspicions about Biggles' intellect had been sharpened when on his first morning on the job he'd turned up wearing odd shoes, a black one and a brown one. His excuse, that he'd dressed hurriedly in the dark, alerted the Senior Sequencer to the fact that someone had arrived in his squad who might just be capable of giving his ulcer an ulcer.

Cutter was sitting at his desk, checking through a bundle of specification tallies, and being made jumpy by the silence of his phone (it'd been ringless for over two minutes), when the beast began its 'lift me' clamour. He obeyed with a resigned sigh. Mal Kibbley's voice began to chafe Cutter's eardrum. Grim news: in the guise of a Geneva Show Car, the SM intended to run a Poacher through the system. The job number would be S4. The workforce were to be kept in the dark; if they got wind of the fact that the car was for a pal of the SM's then they'd have the Stubbs farce all over again. Cutter began to doodle tiny gibbets and guillotines on his notepad. Etched indelibly into his memory was the legend of Horace Stubbs, MP's Salamander. This had been a special-build job that'd foundered on the line, prey to sabotage and petty reprisals, because Stubbs, while serving as a local councillor, had seen fit to single out the Centaur workforce in a newspaper article as being a 'strike-happy bunch of industrial misfits whose arrogance was matched only by their indolence'.

Later, and most certainly because he'd been elected as parliamentary candidate in the Centaur heartland, Stubbs had sought to stitch up his ravelled political image there by ordering a Centaur Salamander, announcing this publicly, and, at the same time, admitting that perhaps he'd been in error to 'condemn the entire engine because of a few dodgy spark plugs'.

Such sentiments did nothing to save Stubbs's Salamander as it began its reconciling run down the build-lines. In Broadmoor the car-shell got crushed on the transit lines. Its replacement weathered a series of malicious welds but on reaching the paint shop was sprayed the wrong colour, resprayed, then finally, after some wild trucking by Basher Bradleigh, it'd been wrapped around a steel post in the trim shop. And so it'd gone on, until by the time Stubbs' Mark 3 version had finally got to the sales compound, it could scarcely be seen for protective snipes. Stubbs' Salamander had passed into plant folklore as an episode in which more heads had rolled than during the entire French Revolution.

'You want what?' Cutter barked into the mouthpiece. Kibbley repeated himself. Cutter's face took on a coronary sheen. 'Where the hell'm I to find an intelligent sequencer? Shaved baboons – that's all personnel keeps sending me. Hold on, here's the king of the tree-swingers, himself!' Cutter looked up at the drooling Biggles. 'Okay,' he groaned, 'tell's the worst – you've gone'n shipped a bloody stacker-truck. Am I close?'

Biggles grinned, then shook his head. 'There's a "roofer" on track only it's not.'

'What?'

'Got its hat on. Y'know, they haven't slapped no vinyl on it.' Biggles scratched his wet chin. 'Beats me how it got on track. Guess I must've been on my break . . .'

'See Telfer,' Cutter said. 'Tell'm to sub it with the "roofer" on the Loop.'

Biggles trudged from the office.

'The Brain of Britain, himself,' Cutter said into the phone.

Kibbley sighed. 'What's he done this time?'

'He's the very man for the S4 job.'

While Kibbley was climbing back onto his chair, Cutter made a quick sketch of a clown pulling a toy model of a Deluxe Sultan along on a piece of string. He'd time to print S4 on its doors before the flabbergasted Martian was able to resume speech, or what passed for it – a series of squeaks which suggested that he'd suffered a sex-change.

'Yeah, I know all that,' Cutter said. 'He couldn't find his arse'n a fog, not even if he'd a bell tied to it. Sure, that's true, but look at it this way . . .' Kibbley listened as if his life depended on it – which it did, well, his working one, anyway. Because the sequencer squad worked a duty-rostering system, next week Biggles would be in Broadmoor. The very thought of the calamities that could flow from this made his napehair bristle: mis-sequenced car-shells being mangled in the gates; auto-monsters – American right-hand-drive models crawling to birth; maybe (who could say it was beyond such a cretin?) the grotesque marriage of a Sultan to a Salamander! Some nights Kibbley woke up gibbering as the vision returned to him of four Sultans riding the high track together although the man-assignments mix clearly called for them to be separated by intervening Salamanders. When such a faux-pas occurred, The Widow's ops showed no mercy – they simply blacked the mis-sequenced cars, letting them go on an unprofitable ride around the build circuit before they'd forlornly arrive back in the trim shop where they'd await reassignment to the high-track. What, Cutter was now asking, did the S4 job entail? Merely that a sequencer should accompany it through all of its build-stages, and report its progress, or – heaven forbid! – its lack of it, at frequent intervals. It was a nothing job. But it included a bonus – the fact that a nitwit like Biggles should be allowed to ride shotgun with the 'show-car' would avert curiosity, drop it down many notches in importance.

After much demurring, Kibbley decided to buy it. But, on one vital condition, of course – Cutter would carry the can if there was any foul-up. Cutter agreed. Right now he was carrying more cans than a Heinz conveyor-belt – what difference could one more make?

'Remember,' Kibbley warned, 'Mum's the word on this job. Under no circumstances have the punters to twig it's a Poacher. Right?'

'Right.' Morosely, Cutter dropped the squawker into its cradle, where it was allowed to slumber for all of five seconds before being roused once more. The sepulchral tones of Tombstone Telfer chilled Cutter's ear.

'This shithead, Biggles, claims you want a sub looped around the roof. But he's not sure whether you wanted a Polaris sub or a Yankee one.'

'He's a subnormal, loopy bastard, and you can tell'm I said so,' barked Cutter. 'I'll be with you'n a minute, Norrie.' Cutter cracked the receiver down and, instantly, it began to ring. He lifted the exasperating thing and slammed it into a drawer.

'I'm hearing,' said Badger Brent, 'there's a Poacher on-track.'

'A Poacher, eh? S'that so?'

O'Hara was so taken by the news that he didn't bother to look up from his copy of the KIKBAK, the rag everybody, including the boilerhouse cat, knew he'd a hand in.

Brent took a gulp from his tea mug. 'Gebbie was telling me.'

O'Hara held up the Xeroxed page. 'Was Belle half-on when she typed this? Talk about bloody Chinese!'

'Machine's knackered,' Brent said. 'Drops more letters than a puggled postie.'

'Fucksake!' O'Hara exclaimed. 'She's only gone'n missed that chunk about the safety-man's accident!'

They were sitting in a snack area that flanked the final line. Completed cars, soon to be released from The Widow's steely embrace, drifted past.

The rectification area, or 'crapyard', as it was more familiarly known, was poxed with cars that were flagged with inspection cards denoting shortages, on-track damage, and blemishes of one kind or another, the outcome of down-quality work on the nightshift. A couple of Suits from the audit team were climbing all over a Sultan estate and didn't look happy about what they were finding.

'Maybe we should do a clamp number on it. What d'you think?'

'Mm, about what?'

'The Poacher!' Brent flared up. 'How about listening for a change?'

O'Hara still didn't give him his full attention. With his eyes skimming the KIKBAK's fuzzy print, he murmured: 'So, there's a Poacher on track? Big deal!'

'It's being run for a Martian.'

The handout was lowered. 'Who?'

'In the top five 'cording to Gebbie.'

'And it's definitely a Poacher?'

Brent nodded. 'Yeah, a basic Sultan. But it'll pick up more extras than The Ten Commandments.'

'How'd Gebbie get onto it?'

'Had the whisper from an analyst.'

O'Hara shook his head. 'Probably just a show job.'

'No way!' declared Badger. 'D'you know Chuck Burns, the chaser?'

'Long sideburns, big hooter?'

'Yeah, that's'm. Well, seems he was bevvying with Tommy Cruden from car sales . . .'

O'Hara heard out the rumour, but by the time Badger was through with his story he remained sceptical. 'Okay,' he said, 'they're going to fake a show job; it's not the first time. But why give a retarded roach like Biggles Blane the leash?'

'Camouflage?' suggested Brent.

'Maybe you're right.' O'Hara fired a fag. 'Never

have liked them bastard'n Poachers. I mean, they come down the line hoovering up all the goodies: everything from velour seat covers to fancy wheel trims, not forgetting multi-welds'nd carrying more paint than the Sioux Nation on the fuck'n warpath!' O'Hara shook his head. 'Industrial abuse, that's what it is, Brother. Shouldn't be allowed. Ought to be stopped.'

Badger Brent nodded. 'Yeah – but stopped where?'

O'Hara tilted his head and let the smoke drift from his mouth. 'I think,' he said, 'I'll have a wee chat with Ironhead Hansen . . .'

The instruction given by Cutter to Biggles Blane was rudely precise: 'Stick to that car like your arse was welded to it!'

Biggles complied so literally to his Senior Sequencer's order that an exasperated-sounding greyback got on the horn to Cutter: 'That Geneva Show Car you're running . . .'

Cutter's heart began to biff his ribs. 'What about it?'

'You'd best get round here'nd sort out your guy. Seems the brainless bugger wants to go through the ovens with it.'

During its paintshop journey Cutter received many anxious phone calls from Kibbley, demanding updates on the Poacher's progress. To everyone in the know's surprise the S4 job emerged unscathed from the paint shop and proceeded to the trimline, its natty Sundance Red body parcelled in protective paper wrapping, its Geneva Show Car tabs conspicuously displayed.

Biggles plodded faithfully alongside his charge as it

approached the glass-line section. Sometimes he stuck so closely to his task he got jostled by the operators. 'Hey, Fergie!' shouted one to his greyback. 'Get this fuck'n penguin off my toes!'

Biggles again got too close to the working area as the S4 inched through the glass-line and Ironhead Hansen, a colossus whose muscles looked sheathed in boilerplate, and whose bald head had been known to unhinge doors, fetched'm a hearty whack across his shoulders with a window as he swung around to engage it with a car's rear aperture. No apology came from Ironhead's grinning lips as he malletted the window into place. Biggles, who'd at least enough sense to realise that rabbits don't take on combine-harvesters, meekly removed his compound-smeared jacket and tried to sponge it clean with some white spirits he'd found in a can at the trackside.

It was shortly after this – when the S4 had passed into the headliners' area – that the fire-klaxon was triggered.

With exultant whoops the ops rapidly deserted their work zones; they spilled from the high track, from the seats section, the vinyl roofing area, the trimline and the underseal section, a rowdy, jostling mob of white-boilersuited men, baying like kids who'd been allowed to split early from kindergarten. After ten or so seconds, the demanned Widow came to what seemed a grudging halt.

Greybacks scurried around, ensuring by reference to their crewsheets that their squads had quit the building. Doors were slid or slammed shut, especially those of the paint hospital where the fire was thought to be located.

The men stood in the chilly yard, relishing this unforeseen deliverance from the tracks. The ops chatted and smoked, and already an impromptu kickabout with a ball, improvised from rags and masking tape, was underway.

Biggles stood with some of his fellow sequencers bemoaning the state of his jacket. The squad grinned to each other over their cigarettes, and offered scant sympathy. Sam Gates, one of the telex sequencers, said that Biggles should count himself lucky that Ironhead hadn't set about'm with his mallet.

No one was more relieved than Steve Laker, the new-start, when the fire turned out to be a false alarm. It would have been an irony indeed if after Stella, his wife, had declared a truce the Plant had gone up in smoke. He already hated the job, especially the scandalous conditions, but at least it paid their mounting bills.

The greybacks came to recall their respective squads into the building. Ed Shirren, the controller, logged the restart time but wasn't too surprised when The Widow came to a halt again. The new stoppage was more'n likely down to the headliners, for it was at their section that the button'd gone in. A notoriously bolshie lot, they always milked every stoppage, extending its duration for as long as possible. But Shirrin was flabbergasted when their greyback, Fergie Farquarson, phoned to tell'm that the stoppage was down to a labour dispute – a complete walk-off by the headliners.

When he was told what the beef was Shirrin's jaw dropped open.

'Say that again!' he squawked.

'Some dirty swine's shat in the show car!'

It proved to be a black hour for the CIA (Centaur Industrial Arbitration). The glass-line shoppies said there was no way their men were going to work the car while the 'offensive object' remained within it. An exasperated Ted Bullock summoned the janitorial greyback and told'm to get one of his men pronto to the show car with shovel, brush and disinfectant. But not one of the bog men was willing to comply. Keeping a straight face, their shoppy said that their remit was to clear human waste from toilets but from nowhere else.

Soon the trim shop janitorial force, like the head-liners, was 'off-the-clock'. The affair, which had at first been treated as a real hoot, began to take a more serious turn when a rumour circulated to the effect that the entire labour force was on the verge of being sent up the road. Union representation was beefed up to a more senior level as the meeting in the CIA office continued. Recriminations began to burn down telephone wires. How'd it been possible that the greybacks in the affected area hadn't spotted the operator doing what'd been done in the show car? Much stress was laid on the words 'show car', as if to imply that had the dirty deed been done in a humble Salamander then the offence would've been less heinous.

In their defence the greybacks claimed that 'the object' had been produced elsewhere – probably by Skunky Scanlan was one suggestion – then planted in the car during the fire evacuation. A proposal put by the union, namely, that the show car should be removed from the track temporarily and subbed by another Sultan was, surprisingly, vetoed by the Bull. Seemingly he'd been warned from on high that the show car was under no circumstances to be taken off-track. Cutter received plenty of phone calls, none of which were pitched at the same hysterical level as Mal Kibbley's. He demanded to know why his man, despite the fire alarm, hadn't waited until the very last moment before deserting his post? That had been his brief, had it not? After similar ravings, Cutter was told to bring his man over to Kibbley's office, and to be 'toot sweet' about it! 'And, by the way,' the Martian added, 'I trust you remember that putting Biggles in charge of the S4 was your idea?'

Cutter headed for the bothy where the sequencer squad usually played cards during production downtime. But Biggles wasn't amongst them. He phoned the telex office; he wasn't there either. It was only after he'd checked out the seats' snack area that it dawned on'm where he'd be. And, sure enough, there he was, arms folded across his chest, brow creased as if in deep thought – although, if you stepped into Biggles' mind it wouldn't have come past your ankles – faithfully guarding the S4 job on the static line.

'We've to go across to the office,' Cutter told'm, then added: 'Don't expect to come back with your plums intact!'

'It must've happened when I was on my break,' Biggles said, saliva juicing his lips.

Cutter shook his head. 'I shouldn't try to –' He paused, the significance of what Biggles was pointing to beginning to sink in. What felt like frozen tongs roughly prodded for his ulcer, locating, then grabbing it in their closing steely jaws.

'My God!' gasped Cutter, as he stooped to run his fingers along the deep scars some sharp tool had gouged through the car's multi paint layers before digging into the underlying metal itself.

'Least there's one consolation,' mumbled Biggles.

'What's that?' the stricken Cutter panted, as in the pit of his stomach the tongs squeezed all the more fiercely.

Biggles paused to wipe his gelatinous lips with the back of his hand before answering: 'At least they'd only time to do the passenger door on the other side!'

O'Hara was studying a shortage card in the crapyard when Badger Brent approached him. Shaking his head, he tucked the S/C under the windscreen wiper of the Salamander he'd been inspecting. 'Y'know,' he said, 'it's amazing the rubbish they're building these days. Just not trying a leg.'

Behind Brent he could see the cars sailing towards the off-ramp. The Widow had started up as soon as the damaged S4 had been declared a non-runner. On and on it pushed the cars like they were so many coloured beads on an abacus. Today, a wire on that abacus had snapped and sixty or so Martian minutes had irretrievably spilled.

'Listen,' Badger said, as O'Hara moved to appraise a Sultan estate's list, 'I can get evens that the next Poacher'll not even make it to the paint shop.'

'Not bad odds,' an impressed O'Hara murmured. 'I think I'll have a slice of that myself . . .'

---

OBITCHERY                    ALEXANDER MCWHUSSLE (66)

---

The death is announced of Sandy McWhussle, the dearly
beloved bit-on-the-side of Ella Choppers.  He leaves a
cheering, sorry a grieving widow and ten children
('those in Swaziland not counted.)'
    McWhussle was born in Ahuri - a small townlet in the
Grampians, which is famous for its tartan, hand-kniitted
sheep.
    Only recently retired from Centaur Cars (Chimeford)
U.K. where he was a time clerk in its framing shop, Mc
whussle actuallystarted his lifelong auto career in
Coventry, where the legendary "Centaur Seraph" made its
historic debut.
    Mc Whussle was in his late thirties when he made his
move to yet another of the Centaur's " Trans-plants"
this one being based at the sleepy rural hamlet of
Chimeford.
    It was McWhussle who founded the "Flippin' Hecks"
- an awesome tiddly-winks combo that won everything
winnable before they were tragically drowned during a
midnight romp in a hotel pool when their raft foundered
on a duck This of course, produced the famous sportng
headline: "DUCK SINKS TIDDLY "WINKS" DURING MIDNIGHT
HIGH JINKS!"
    McWhussle will also be long-remembered for his
innovative attempt to introduce oxygen into MAD, but
despite the fact that he was unsuccessful in this
enterpride, he did persuade the Martians to accept
that shackling mainline ops to their assigned working
areas was totlaly unnecessary and their acknowledgement
of this marked a major landmark in the Centaur workforces
emancipation from slavery.  It as for this reason that
McWhussle was affectionately known as the " ABe Lincoln
of the Automobile Industry".
    Plans are now being made to launch a McWhussle Fund

with which it is hoped to sponsor any up and coming
young alcoholic Centaur is almost certain to produce in
the very near future.
        (See Press for funeral details.  No Flowers please,
but bank-notes of all demominations will be most acceptable.)


                        A MUSEUM PIECE.
The fact that the National Transport Museum saw fit to
take possession of a Series 1. Centaur Seraph, should not
come as a surprise.
        "It's a splendid acquisition" said the Musuem's curator.
"This car,you know, was built almost entirely by hand"
        What's he think we use nowadays - our feet!"

# The
# Widow's
# Bite!

Since they were the trim-line shoppies, it fell to Billy
Spiers and Dixie Donnigan to take up a cash collection
from their respective shifts on behalf of the late Henry
Wormsley's widow. The Worm's fatal coronary attack
had been the latest in a freak spate of sudden deaths
amongst trim shop operators. Consequently, Billy
Spiers, the nightshift shoppy, had had a thin time of it
as he'd toured the lines with bereavement sheet'nd
collection box.

Discussing the matter with Donnigan in the locker-
room as the nightshift interchanged with the oncoming
dayshift, he'd shaken his head. 'A waste of time, Dixie.
Ten pee short of a tenner. If you do as poorly we'd be as
well calling it a day and giving the punters their dough
back.'

Spiers, having wriggled from his boilersuit, stuck it

into his locker along with his tea mug and an Ed McBain paperback. Before slamming the door shut he unhooked his anorak and with flailing arms swam into the bulky garment. The zip-fastener's teeth intermeshed with a metallic chirring sound as Spiers hauled up its lug. Both shoppies now began to edge their way through the throng of ops who were either donning or shucking their boilersuits, their voices already beginning to rise to shouting pitch to compensate for the racket of early a.m. chit-chat and locker-door slamming.

Having left the locker area, Spiers, in a voice half-strangled by a yawn, asked: 'Is it a chimney or a spade job, then?'

'Neither,' Dixie said.

'So, what's left – DIY Embalming?'

'Wormsley donated his body to medical research.'

'Well, that should set it back a year'nd plenty.'

Another yawn cratered Spiers' face. 'Man,' he said, 'am I bushed! Telling you, I'm gonna give that pillow some heavy-duty ear-bashing.' He shook his head: 'See nightshift, Dixie – fit only for owls and prostitutes, and that's a fact.'

Donnigan soon got a taste of the ops' resentment when, having obtained the reluctant go-ahead from Phil Sprake, his greyback, he appeared in their midst with bereavement sheet and collection box, ready to put the 'Widow's Bite' on them. Doc Snoddy, a Sultan fog-lamp fitter's, response was fairly typical: 'Chrissake Dixie, what gives? Guys're dropping faster'n drawers in a knocking shop. Telling you, if this keeps up we'll have to take out insurance cover.'

Roofer Billy Butters, his gun spraying a fine mist of glue across a clipped and tautly clamped spread of tan vinyl, laconically warned, 'Y'know, Dixie, you can go to the well once too often.'

His mate, Pete Perkins, reluctantly chucked a fifty-pence piece into Donnigan's collection box, saying as he did so, 'Just'n case the ugly wee turd comes back to haunt me!'

It didn't take Dixie long to accept that he wasn't going to do any better than his nightshift counterpart. In fact, it began to look as if he'd be lucky to even drum up a tenner. Whenever he approached a section it'd immediately begin to shed ops quicker'n fleas desert a dead mutt. On this or that pretext – a toilet break; a sick-bay visit; using any excuse at all – they made themselves scarce, much to the disgruntlement of the relief men and snaggers who were drafted in by their greybacks as cover during their ops' absence.

It was something of a bonus for Donnigan when he was actually approached by a punter proffering a pound coin, although each time the shoppy reached to take it, the op mischievously whisked it away.

'Helluva lean takings you've there, Dixie. Hardly enough to buy the widow some nose-wipes.'

Donnigan made a grab for the ubiquitous coin but failed again to grasp it. The tease-merchant was Gus Gebbie, a plant-wide garbage collector (an apt job for Centaur's most prolific gossip), a man who'd been succinctly described as 'a guy with keen sense of rumour'.

Gus Gebbie was a small man, as quick as a greased otter, with a frisky talent for surfacing from even the drabbest stream of events with a juicy red herring wriggling in his gob. Lies, exaggeration, distortion, innuendo, all were as natural to Gebbie as were lumps to canteen custard. So expert was he in the art of fact-bending that anyone in the plant judged to be tarting up the truth would soon hear the time-honoured phrase: 'Don't come the Gebbie!' It was a safe bet that if the Martians wanted a rumour leaked onto the shop floor, they'd advise their agent: 'Get this to Gebbie!'

The scandalmonger now drew Donnigan into the passageway that ran parallel to the trimline, distancing them some from the uproar of storeline shunts and the bedlam of on-track operations.

'So The Worm croaked from a blitzed beater, eh?' Gebbie's head wagged. 'They didn't have to unzip'm to learn that.'

'It's the law, Gus. Must have a PM if the death's sudden.'

'Sudden? You're jesting. Those lips of his – you saw'm – blue they was, like he'd been chawing on a snooker cube, or swigging ink.' Gebbie nodded. 'A sure sign – see that'n a geezer's fish'n chips and its odds-on he'll soon be kissing the cobbles.'

Tantalisingly, the coin continued to spin beyond Donnigan's grasp.

The garbage-humper leaned closer to bawl in his ear: 'Heard he was found belly-up outside a fishmonger's shop. S'that right?'

Donnigan shrugged.

Gebbie began to prattle about the deceased having been of the Jewish faith.

'Baloney! If The Worm was a Jew then Hitler was a Hottentot.'

' "Shoes", I said, not Jews. He was found minus his clogs. The Plods say that they was snaffled by an old down'nd out, name of Stogie Joe, who kips in a wardrobe down Lepers' Lane. Natch, them Plods want to know how the decrepit dosser, who's well-known to them, came to acquire such a nifty pair of puddle-hoppers instead of his usual battered old boots that were held together with twine and industrial tape.

'Eventually, Stogie owns up to've taken the shoes from the dead Wormsley. "There he was, stretched out along the fishmonger's step. I'm telling it straight, fellas, I never seen such an ugly stiff, never'n all my born days . . ."

'But the Plods don't buy this story; they threaten him with more of their off-the-wall, machine-made coffee, and Stogie Joe cracks. He now admits that, yes, when he'd first laid lamps on'm, the ugly bugly had still been sucking air, though it was plenty obvious that his tank was running close to dry. "As I got nearer to'm, doesn't he haul off one of his St Louis Blues. His bunions must've been biting real fierce, for once he'd hauled off the how-d'you-do? this look of total relief hits his pan, like he's just had a litre of morphine needled up his buns.

' "Well, he goes on squatting there, and all the time he's tumbling the shoe over'nd over between his forks till he finds the which-way to catch the most light from the overhead street lamp. Next, like he's trying to screw up nerve, he sucks in a deep breath, then takes a long hard stare into the shoe.

' "Suddenly, the guy cuts loose with a weird kind of wailing noise like a moggie's apt to make when it wakens to find itself halfway down the throat of a Rottweiler. You'd've thought to hear'm that he'd found a scorpion in 'is Dan Magroo. Whatever it was, he obviously wanted no part of it, for with another groan he chucks away the Dr Who, which by fluke lands in the lidless fishbin.

' "Next, he hauls off 'is other Dr Who, only, this time, he's so tuckered out that when he flings the shoe it drops yards short of the bin. Now, boys, I admit I'm no Doc, but when I hear a guy apanting and agroaning like this poor gink was doin', even I knowed he'd hardly more'n a few sups of life left to'm. I thought of calling an ambulance for there's a phonebox real handy but, blow me, didn't I go'n forget the hurry-hurry number! Boy, was I ever pissed off with myself! I knew the first three digits was 999, but when it came to the fourth figure I was lost down a mine with a gassed canary. No point either in trying to shake the lost digit outa the guy on the deck, the poor bugger'd troubles enough, waiting for his cardiac to arrest itself. Anyway, who's to say he wanted help? I mean he'd been toting that mongrel-face around for so long maybe he was ready to have it put down.

' "You're probably thinking I'm making excuses. I don't blame you for that, but when you see a guy chucking away his Fair-dos in the street, well, you don't have to've dead-heated at *Mastermind* to figure that his wandering days are over: could it be any clearer? 'Show me the exit, pal,' that's what he's saying, 'I've had my fill of this walking-up-and-down stuff.' "

'So, old Stogie Joe, having tried on the Sierra Sioux that lay near the bin and finding it to be a snug fit, was forced to scarper when his crime-trained ears picked up the sound of a speedily approaching Plod Panda. Seizing the binned shoe, he stole away from the dying man, who was risking pneumonia, never mind pleurisy, by lying on the fishmonger shop's wet steps.'

His fellow dossers – about five wretches in all – had stirred neither body nor tongue, hadn't even spared him so much as a glance when he came into their midst proffering a dead man's uneaten meal. He placed the sandwich-crammed lunchbox before a ragged man known as Toeless Tony, although all of his toes were intact.

The man took the late Henry Wormsley's lunchbox and cast it into the flames. As the writhing plastic began to spurt rainbow smokes, Stogie Joe had risen from his semi-crouching stance, and as stealthily as Dracula returning from a night of gore-hunting, retreated to his lair.

Once he was safely bolted within his wardrobe, Joe'd settled down to enjoy the novelty of a long overdue gloat. His arduous life, it was true to say, had been a singularly gloatless one and perhaps Stogie Joe, who'd been booted in the butt so often by Fate, should've known better'n to've entertained the notion that there might just be after all a smidgin of justice to be had on this ball of mud they called a planet. But Stogie'd been decidedly miffed ("fuckn fuming" were the exact words he'd used in the interview room of the cop-shop in Cooler Street) to find he'd been suckered yet again.

Externally the shoes were exact mirror images of

each other. Joe was able to confirm this by the light from his battery-operated lamp, a light source he made only the most frugal use of since, like himself, its batteries were running low on juice. Lying there on his back he was able to spectate on his ungoverned fury in his very own wardrobe's looking-glass. He could hear too the echoes of his curses as he thrust and thrust his foot into the left shoe. But it proved hopeless; at a pinch he could squash it on, but like a torturer's Iron Boot that single pinch would father a thousand new ones.

So, the shoes that'd seemed a perfect match, a marriage cobbled in heaven, had turned out to be anything but: a glance into the shoes soon revealed why; yes, it was true that the inner heels of both shoes depicted the similar comic illustration of a whale. It was also the case that they showed the same merry mammal spouting its manufacturer's trademark, while balancing a beachball on its snout; not an iota of difference to be seen. Nevertheless, there was a difference – a whopper! Both buoyant spheres were tabbed by different size numbers, the left one being an 8; the right one a size 9.

But, since he was a man of dogged stubbornness, Stogie didn't just leave matters there. No, instead he took himself on a pre-dawn safari in the vain hope that he might be able to stretch the pinching left shoe by wriggling his foot about in its cramping interior. It was while he was doing this, limping around in the smoke-like rain, that a car had hissed up alongside'm and its driver'd invited him for a coffee and a cigarette in the comfort of the Cooler Street nick.

Donnigan shook his head'n admiration. 'Gotta

hand it to you, Gus, you told that like you was there, personally, taking it all down in shorthand. How d'you do it? That's what I'd like to know.'

'It's a gift, that's all,' said a modest Gebbie. 'A natural talent. Course, in this instance the fine shading's down to my brother, Bruce.'

'Your brother? Where'd he fit in?'

'Bruce? Well, he's on the civvy staff in the cop shop, ain't he? On the phones, mostly, but sometimes when there's not much doing on the crime front he's been known to earn himself a pack of ciggies by typing up crime scene reports for them fumble-fingered Plods. With me?'

Donnigan nodded as a major piece of the enigma that was Gus Gebbie – where did the guy source his inside info? – dropped neatly into place. 'Receiving you loud'n clear. Now, how'd you like to settle that pound you got there in favour of the widow Wormsley?'

Gebbie promptly dropped his pound into the shoppy's box but diminished his donation by withdrawing a fifty-pence piece which he flicked into the air then deftly caught.

'Did The Worm've any sprogs?' he enquired, determined, it seemed, to extract as much info as poss in return for his contribution.

Donnigan shook his head, passing the sheet and pen to Gebbie.

'I figured not,' said Gebbie. 'A right ugly wee sod, eh? Made the Elephant Man look like Clark Gable. His wife must've been either blind or desperate.' Gebbie signed the sheet then, with a quick flourish, he returned it to Donnigan.

'C'mon, Gus, that's how I got it.'

With a smirk, Gebbie surrendered the pen. He grabbed the shoppy's arm, delaying his departure. 'Have you heard anything on the redundancy, Dixie?'

Donnigan shook his head.

'They've done for the lint-heads like I told you they would.' Gebbie nodded. 'Them ay-rabs shat'n their own nest. Too much anti-Yank booing, too little car screwing. Yup, them "Gate-Slammers" jetted in and junked 'em.'

Still clutching Donnigan's arm, Gebbie ludicrously affected a secretive air, as if he was anxious that the great secret he was about to impart should be heard only by the shoppy himself, whereas, given the racket being made by the trim-line, plus the shattering uproar a fitter was arousing with a heavy-duty drill as he replaced a damaged floor rail in the car-shell storage area, not forgetting the far from delicate trucking of Basher Leighton, who was busily creating his usual, high-decibel tumult as his machine repeatedly rammed the model-lines, there was no more likelihood of Gebbie being overheard than there was of Tombstone Telfer's lips carrying a smile longer'n ten seconds.

'I'm hearing, too, Dixie, that the Centaur dagos are for the long siesta. The best them Bilbao bums can hope for's a few hundred ops to run a screwdriver outfit.' His hand dropped from Donnigan's arm. 'But it's just as bad for us, Dixie – we're for the kibosh soon: full nightshift wipe-out! That's kosher.'

Donnigan stepped away a pace or so from the incorrigible rumour-monger. He shook his head.

'Know what I think, Gus? I think maybe you're reading too many KIKBAKS.'

Gebbie grinned and yanked on his tattered gloves. 'I'll keep you a place in the dole queue, Dixie.' With this parting remark Centaur's ace-stirrer clambered onto his garbage truck'nd, with a couple of gruff horn honks, drove off.

Donnigan, in no hurry to resume his track duties, ambled to the far end of the trim shop, passing amongst the crates of yellow foam-rubber stacked one on top of the other like huge slabs of cheese. These laden crates formed dark higgledy-piggledy passage-ways, most of which petered out in shadowy cul-de-sacs, thickly felted with dust and spattered with bird droppings. Threading his way through this maze, Donnigan was stopped short by a sight that had his credulity spinning faster'n a straw hat'n a gale. There, cutting themselves a wedge of passion cake, lip-to-lipping, and, by the looks of it, fast-tracking to some hip-to-hipping, was the most hilarious sextogether Donnigan had ever laid eyes on. Not even Gene Autry making it with Ol' Mother Riley, or Bette Davis having a three'n-a-bed romp with Stan'n Olly, could've topped the bizarre mating he'd stumbled upon. An Amazon and a pygmy – none other than Delilah Hansen, wife of the fearsome Ironhead Hansen, and, of all people, Midge Stacey was her incongruous partner! An intrigued Dixie sought out a vantage point behind some crates where he could watch unobserved a feat that should've been physically impossible – Tom Thumb having a knee-trembler with Snow White sprang to mind. Despite being scarcely four feet in height, Midge, it was rumoured, packed a sex-cannon that would've made even Errol Flynn's legendary endowment look like a Derringer pistolette. Nature's extravagant compensation for Midge Stacey's lack of stature had passed into Centaur's jokelore and had become the obsessive subject of skunkbox graffiti. On this occasion, the resourceful and randy midget had overcome his height disadvantage by standing on an upended crate, after having insulated his partner from bruising as well as granting an erotic resilience to their ecstatic buffetings by packing chunks of foam-rubber behind her spine'nd buttocks. Being a touch sadistic, not to mention a whole hunk envious, Donnigan deliberately waited until the odd but decidedly ardent twosome were only a few hip thrusts from carnal meltdown before he stormed their lovenest.

With all the soul-sundering shock suffered by Faust, the Devil's plaything, when Mephisto-whatsit came roaring up through a floorcrack like a bust gas main, waving, as he did so, his asbestos IOU, so Midge Stacey and Delilah were similarly riven to their randy cores when Donnigan suddenly materialised before them, wagging his finger-stained bereavement sheet and gleefully rattling his collection box.

It was unlikely that either of the lust-locked pair managed to take in Dixie's apology. 'Oops! So sorry – catch you folks later!'

With that he made his way from the maze, leaving the lovers to adjust their clothing and to regroup their jigsawed emotions as best they could. Donnigan, who'd begun loudly to whistle the Tom Jones ditty, 'Delilah', fancied he heard a sort of thumping sound emanating from the trysting area. Maybe it was the midget's coitus suffering a severe interruptus as he toppled from his height-boosting perch.

Meanwhile, there was no let-up in the resistance to Donnigan's sheet. He bumped into Tantamount Oslake, a shop steward from the machine shop, who immediately began to chide'm on the grounds that, according to a recent directive from Union H.Q., bereavement-sheet collections were to be discouraged.

'I mean,' Oslake said, 'it's tantamount to encouraging back-sliders to neglect their death-cover obligations. Tell me this, Dixie: why should shoppies have to take all that snash the punters dish out? I's just not on! If you ask me, it's tantamount to implying that we're in for a cut of the takings ourselves. Don't you agree?'

Before Donnigan had the chance to speak, Tantamount's mouth was back in action. 'Anyway, from what I hear, The Worm's widow's not short of a bob or two. For starters, she's the manageress of a shoe shop in Main Street. Just the same, that didn't stop'r from making the goblin go on constant nightshift, not to mention having him to work as gardener, decorator, window-cleaner and what-not. Another thing, I bet she's got plenty of insurance moolah riding on his five-cornered skull.' Oslake nodded. 'You can be sure of one thing – that shrewd bitch won't ever have to pop'r weasel up there'n Hooker Heights to square the rent.'

One of the trim-line jokers, Mo Sutton, was arousing some cheap sniggers by stuffing a bundle of cotton waste up the back of his boilersuit to simulate a hump, then, with a sleeve emptily dangling, he twisted his face into a parody of Charles Laughton's grotesque impression of Quasimodo, though it was evident to all, as he shambled along behind Donnigan, eyes violently rolling, tongue dangling from between his slavering lips, who the subject was really intended to be.

After a further three knockbacks and with a sum so measly – counting the nightshift's tenner, it came to about seventeen quid – Donnigan'd begun to consider scrubbing the collection and returning the dough to the punters. Tantamount Oslake was right. It was bad enough being made to feel like an accomplice in what KIKBAK, in one of its more serious moods, referred to as 'These industrial serial killings, this passionless wasting of our sisters and brothers on the dollar-scarred anvil of capitalist profit', without having to take all the sarky crap the trim shop ops dished out to him when he approached with his sheet and collection box. Mo Sutton's parody was maybe the last straw, although this'd come to an abrupt ending when Phil Sprake, the greyback, arrived on the scene.

'C'mon, Sutton,' he said crossly, 'at least try to hide the fact that you're an asshole.' As he was saying this his hand was simultaneously locking onto Donnigan's boilersuit sleeve, and effectively curtailing the shoppy's attempt to quietly vamoose. Donnigan was forced to stand there, abjectly tethered to Sprake, while the greyback got pitched into the prankster.

It was about a fortnight later – it seemed that long to the pissed-off Donnigan – before the greyback concluded his lecture. It'd obviously made no impression on Sutton, who was a ringer for Mo of The Three Stooges, especially so now with a dim-witted smirk flexing his rubbery-looking lips. To titters from his amused workmates, Sutton retrieved his trim-line tools from relief man 'Laughing' Larry Studmann, who, despite his nickname, was about as funny as a bombed crêche, and a fully-paid-up member of the Tombstone Telfer Club.

With the exchange of tools completed, what'd appeared to be a comradely pat turned out to be the means by which Sutton proved able to stick a sheet of sticky paper which bore the vividly felt-tipped legend: 'I AM A DICKHEAD!' to Studmann's back.

Even Phil Sprake, who'd all but talked his gums bald lecturing the rogue, had a struggle to curb a grin.

'D'you see the Poison Dwarf on your travels?' he asked Donnigan.

'Last I saw of'm he was screwing Ironhead Hansen's missus in the foam-rubber store,' Donnigan could've said, but wisely chose not to, for such a statement would've undoubtedly prompted the greyback to have'm whisked round to Dr Mengeles' surgery, where, after he'd blown the dust from his medical pass-out pad, the Doc would've had'm shipped out to Lobotomy Towers.

Donnigan took a quid from his collection box and handed it to the greyback.

'What's this?' asked the mystified Sprake.

'Your donation,' said Donnigan.

'My dough not good enough or something?'

Donnigan shook his head. 'I'm jacking in the collection, Phil. Too much hassle.'

Sprake was not a happy man. 'Hassle? What d'you know about hassle? I've been running up'n down this line plugging more holes than Red Adair sees in a damned fortnight, and you've the nerve to tell me –'

'They're skint, Phil. Too many sheets . . .'

Sprake shook his head. 'I've been jerked around once too often. Anyway, how much dough've you got?'

Donnigan told'm; Sprake humped his shoulders. 'It's not much, maybe, but it's better'n nowt. You've heard of the "Widow's Mite", I suppose?'

Donnigan nodded.

'Good,' said Sprake, although the boring-again Christian looked miffed at being denied the chance to mouth-off a sermon. He tossed the spurned coin back into Donnigan's box.

'Then you'll see that by scrubbing the collection you'd be letting down those who saw fit to contribute. Mind if I take a look?'

Sprake glanced down the name-list. 'Hmm, quite a few missing in action.'

'As you'll recall, we'd a sudden outbreak of dysentery.' Donnigan shook his head. 'There wasn't a vacant skunkbox to be had.'

'Here's one who seems t've recovered.'

Sprake was staring over Dixie's shoulder in the direction of the passageway where Midge Stacey was to be seen driving his forky at a fair lick. As the machine rippled through a roofbeam its blades for an illusionary moment seemed piled with bright planks of sunlight.

'I'll stop 'm – you nab'm.'

So saying, Sprake stepped into the passageway with hand upraised. Stacey was forced to bring his forky to a halt. The midget looked jumpy, probably unsure if Donnigan'd spilled the beans about his amorous encounter with Ironhead Hansen's missus in the foam-rubber store. He looked mightily relieved when Sprake instructed'm to transfer some urgently required materials to the glass-line, and to be quick about it, or they'd have a track-stopper on their hands.

Donnigan moved in swiftly with his money box and the scowling Stacey wrested a pound note from one of his pockets and grudgingly thumped it into the container.

'C'mon, you can do a lot better'n that,' Donnigan winked. 'Even if you were harder up than usual this morning!'

Angrily, Stacey stumped up a further one pound fifty, then, having scrawled his signature on the sheet, took off at a speed that was doubtless prompted more by his concern that Dixie might still want an even greater contribution from him than by the Glass Section's critical materials shortage.

'Well, now, if that don't take the biscuit! What the devil got into him?' exclaimed the dumbfounded Sprake. 'I wouldn't've believed it if I hadn't seen it with my own eyes; he's usually as tight as a frog's bum.'

It was Donnigan's turn to do some sermonising: 'It doesn't always pay to heed factory gossip, Boss. Could be he's got a king-sized heart to match his king-sized peashooter.'

While he was making this comment, Donnigan spotted Delilah Hansen heading into the Soft Trim Area. He left the greyback and crossed the passage to head off Ironhead's spouse.

In a voice that grew louder the closer their respective routes neared convergence, Dixie began to sing, although he would've been the first to admit that his raucous rendition was no challenge to the Welsh Warbler.

'My, my, my, Delilah! Why, why, why, Delilah? . . .'

The recently widowed Martha Wormsley crossed the circular Indian rug which lay like a great iridescent wheel on the lounge's polished parquet flooring. It was highly unlikely that the team of infant weavers whose nimble fingers had produced this tethered rainbow had ever heard a music centre to match the acoustical fidelity of the handsome model the Widow Wormsley was now stooping over. She flipped the beige-labelled LP then, pressing the machine's play button, she stood listening as it went through its delicate preamble of clicks and hums before releasing the record onto the spinning turntable. The pick-up arm glided to the disc's rim then sank its diamond-tipped fang into the groove to rouse a symphonic piece from its dark vinyl slumber.

Martha was well into her middle forties, and looked it. Her blanched features had that peculiar stressed-tissue look that's to be seen on the pampered dials of those vain socialities who've gone one cosmetic op too far. Donnigan felt sure that The Worm's widow had never been under the 'beautifying blade': the exorbitant fees for such exercises in vanity were well beyond what a shoe-shop manageress could afford. No, it was simply Martha Wormsley's misfortune, her fate even, that she looked like she'd lingered overlong on the books of some private cutting agency.

She recrossed the carpet and seated herself once

more on her armchair. Donnigan, ensconced on the matching settee, took another sip from the crystal glass which contained a superb single-malt whisky.

'That's wonderful, isn't it?'

Martha had asked the question as she reached towards the nearby drinks table to take up her Bloody Mary, but instead of taking a sip she sat staring at it as if it was a wayside poppy she'd plucked in the passing. That Donnigan had responded to'r question with a mere nod had apparently not been lost on Martha.

'Henry wasn't too keen on Mahler either,' she said. 'Hated classical music. Preferred the beastly black stuff, y'know, American negro noise.'

She took a sip from her drink, then almost wistfully murmured, 'Poor Henry.'

Donnigan put away some more whisky, which almost immediately had his hostess offering to 'freshen up' his glass. He politely refused her offer, reminding her that he was driving.

'But surely,' she persisted, 'you've time for a cup of tea? It won't take me a mo.'

Donnigan's negative response was cut short by the odd expression that'd suddenly surfaced on Martha's taut face: a sort of startled, perhaps even haunted look it was.

'How strange!'

'You okay?' Dixie asked.

'Y-yes.' She shivered. 'It's just that . . . that Henry used to say that.'

'What?'

' "Won't take a mo." I was always on at'm about his

slang expressions. And now here am I –' She shook'r head again. 'How very odd . . .'

Donnigan had been building up an increasing momentum of departure, preparing himself for the hardest part – presenting the Widow Wormsley with the sheet money – a measly twenty-three quid. Having finished his drink, the glass was to've been a major prop in his leave-taking; it'd been his intention – while muttering some farewell palaver – to've risen and placed the drained glass on the drinks table, leaving the goodbye handshake to the last possible moment, before which, of course, like a card cheat who behind a screen of cigar smoke, small talk, nail-biting, nodding, smiling, bluffing, has been stealthily working his 'poisonous' ace to the top of the deck, Donnigan had likewise been manipulating his pathetically thin money envelope to the surface of events.

Martha Wormsley, however, completely scuppered his escape plan when out of'r clear blue eyes teardrops began to fall. Donnigan couldn't really fault her for this unexpected outburst. No, not even if she'd been unfaithful to the man she was now ostensibly grieving over, the hellishly ugly Henry Wormsley, whom she'd made work harder'n a prospector's mule so that she could relax with her lover, Tommy Tight-Shoe, in this classy lounge, no doubt lying in each other's arms on this very settee, listening enraptured to the symphonic genius of Gustav Mahler, while The Worm, the lover of 'black noise', had been forced – on Martha's instigation – to suffer perpetual owl-shift in the rowdiest area outside the press shop. The widow's breakdown had presented Dixie with a dilemma: should he try to comfort the hag or would it be better to remain silent? Grief born of guilt was usually, in his experience, a short-lived affair. From her sleeve she produced a hanky and began to mop the tears from her stressed face.

'I'm so . . . so sorry about this,' she burbled. 'It's . . . it's so . . . so unlike me . . .'

Donnigan, about to mouth some pious twaddle concerning the injurious effects bottled-up grief can wreak on one's health, rose instead from the settee and, crossing to the drinks table, briskly rapped his drained glass upon it.

'Sorry,' he said to her, 'but I really must go.'

And, true to his words – go he did, right there and then, without even a single pang of conscience at leaving the widow in such a distressed state.

As for the bereavement money problem, why, it solved itself in no time – he just didn't bother to give it to her! Instead, he got into his car and drove to the bottom end of Lepers' Lane. He got out and carefully locked the car before he ventured into the lane itself. His heart was rapping so loudly he was sure it'd be heard by the three dossers who sat with curved backs and melting minds near a hissing fire, having, no doubt, sometime before licked the last precious drops from their bottles of Blue Ruin, and were now on another planet, one that wobbled around some half-assed galaxy that was going nowhere fast.

It didn't take Dixie too long to find Stogie Joe's wardrobe, for he was guided to it by the hacking cough of the man himself.

Donnigan stared down at the wardrobe. It looked

like a decaying coffin half-sunk in mud. He bent and softly rapped on the wardrobe's door and, still wary of the trio of tramps by the fire, he softly called down to Stogie.

'Go away, why don't you? Can't you let an old man die in peace? Quit pestering me. D'you hear?'

Dixie carefully examined the wardrobe and eventually found what he was looking for – a fissure in the lid. He prised this wider by levering at it with his pocket knife until it gaped enough to accommodate the passage of the bereavement-money envelope. He'd to work quickly for Stogie was hollering fit to crack his voice-box and to draw the attention of the other lowlifers who nested hereabouts.

Soon Dixie'd managed to force the envelope through the lid-crevice then jabbed it free with his knife; he heard it drop inside the wardrobe. Stogie Joe ceased his shouting. Some moments later his battery light came on.

Bending close to the wardrobe Dixie shouted: 'It's all yours, Stogie! Try not to blow it all on booze. Save enough for a pair of tough boots. Good luck.'

Donnigan, looking warily about himself, saw a mugger in every shadow, potential cutthroats in each lane recess. It was with a grateful sigh that he saw his car waiting where he'd left it.

Before he drove off, Donnigan paused for some moments and stared down into the dark and desperate place that was Lepers' Lane. God forbid that he'd ever fall so low as to end up there, to become one of its putrid denizens who practised a fierce freemasonry of the damned: 'One for none, and none for all!' A

Buddhahood of the Backlanes – disciples of non-attainment.

Donnigan took off the handbrake, slipped the car into gear, then drove off at such speed you'd've thought he'd the Devil himself on his tail.

## THE MOST EGGCITING EVENT OF THE YEAR!

It had tô happen of course: last week in Centaur's Boßy'n
White Section (That place which is notorious for the dropping
of clangers) an inspector laid an egg! Both egg'nd Inspector were
rushed to the nearby paint ovens were both are said to "be
doing time." "As Chickygrams flooded into the plant from
as far away as Yokeyhama there has been quite a scramble
going on for the inspector's lost overtime.Said one o.t.
hogger:"This is the best clucking thing that's happened
here for a long time.

### PRAY PARDON MY PINCERS!!

There has been a lot of unjustified panic over Centaur Cars'
new disciplinary Procedure.  Rumours that operaotrs have
had their Kit-Kat's confiscated for smoking in the lavs are
completely unfounded.
This assurance was given yesterday by jackbooted, whip carrying
Mr Beltam Harder in his steel panelled office.  Waving
me into his presence he cordially invited me to seat myself
on a broken bottle.
    Next,he passed over a cigar box "Try one of these" he
said  I stretched out my hand and immediatley the lid snapped
up and a small venemous poodle leapt out and bit my fingers.
Harder laughed and fondly tapped his pet with a lead truncheon
" Now then," he asked, foldin his bloodied hands,"What can
I bruise for you?"
I explained the purpose of my visit and when I'd finished he
lobbed a rusty hatchet at me.  "Liked the way you ducked
there" he praised.  "Allow me to show you around.  Just
step over this skeleton here - I was picking a small bone
with'm.

We passed now to a liftman who was being gentley pulled
apart on a rack,his bones splintering merily.."Very shy type
tnis"Harder explained "just can't face up to having people in
his lift.  "We're trying to draw him out a little as you can
see.  Winch'm an inch if you like."

I declined the offer.For a shock even more stunning
than the rest awaited me in the corner.  Behind the blood
smeared bars of a cage I, hardened by Monday mornings as a
snagger on the Widow, saw a squirming revolting heap of near
naked whimpering humans.Hands were raised imploringly  to me
on spaghetti thin arms.Holy Centaur!" I cried. I know these
people. "Then,you should be more careful in your choice of
friends," Harder said grimly ,as he lobbed a half dozen
scorpions and a part-time cobra into their midst.

I left this dungeon of woe and was never so glad to be
back in F.Block withits pigsty pongs and its playful asbestos
blizzards.

# Lazarus
# Thinketh
# Something
# Stinketh!

The raising of Lazarus after his four days of extreme breathlessness must have been a real scroll-scorcher back in Bethany. Unfortunately, how the ex-cadaver got on after he'd received his crypt-transplant isn't recorded, which leaves a myriad of intriguing questions unanswered.

For instance, did those folk who'd enjoyed heavy rakings of boodle from his will have to hand back to'm the amounts remaining thereof? Or had these overjoyed benefactors no sooner heard that Laz'd been sprung from Deadsville than they were hopping on the fastest camels out of town and scampering off to wherever the antique equivalent of Las Vegas had spread its rugs in those days?

And, what about the tomb-dodger, himself? Once the news-hungry scribe-tribe, with their styluses and wax tablets, had quit pestering him for interviews, had he slipped back into his old routine – whatever that was? How long was it before the party invites began to taper off and his wife snappishly insisted that he should wear gloves at mealtimes because the revolting sight of his emaciated, liver-spotted hands would've put a ravenous croc off its chuck? Alas, lacking a follow-up feature, such questions are fated to remain un-answered.

However, no such reporting restrictions attend the case of Curly Brogan, the latterday Lazarus: the facts and rumours concerning this grave-bouncer are prolif-erating faster'n bacteria in a Cairo karzy.

*Centaur Lines,* the Company's official mag, had, amazingly enough, got itself an interesting lead story. Under the headlines:

FEARS INCREASE OF MAJOR SPANISH CLOSURE!

COULD IT BE 'BUENAS NOCHES, BILBAO'?

there followed a highly speculative article that was peppered with bullring jargon, e.g. the builders of the Centaur Segovia weren't so much facing redundancy as they were 'confronting their Moment of Truth!' The Centaur's Bilbao Plant was said to be 'caught on the horns of a dilemma'. Their once nimbly selling 'Centaur Segovia', a spritely hatchback that'd been launched to wide acclaim, had suffered a 'reversal of its fortunes' when two key components faults, both of which affected the braking systems of the Segovia Supreme and Segovia Sports, had necessitated a major recall of both models.

The Segovia never recovered from this double blow

and it was 'badly gored by its competitors in the pitiless arenas of the European car markets'.

Centaur's Detroit-based President, George C. Warrender, had recently been expressing himself with a frankness that was considered by motoring commentators to be imprudent, for, instead of improving the situation, he was unwisely drawing the car-buying public's attention to the Centaur Car Company's parlous financial situation. But, far from heeding such warnings, Warrender had gone even further by declaring at the recent ill-starred Chicago Conference that he intended personally to initiate a most rigorous rationalisation programme which would study with a hawkish and unsparing scrutiny the productivity achievements (or lack of them) of Centaur's European Trans-Plants.

Auto scouts, skilled in the art of reading car-industry smoke signals, proved to be in mutual agreement that the Chicagoan word plume was plainly saying: 'Help! My Poncho's On Fire!'

KIKBAK, despite its crude and downright amateurish production methods, not to mention its clandestine and sporadic extra-mural distribution, consistently scooped its professionally edited, but nonetheless boring rival. This time, though, the *Centaur Lines* editorial team was brimful of confidence that its current issue, which highlighted the plight of the Bilbao car ops, would prove to be an irresistible eye-grabber.

How wide of the mark their forecast proved to be! Not only were they scooped, they were totally eclipsed

– blown clean out of the water – by a devastating torpedo of a headline:

'GRAVE NEWS FOR MARTIANS – CURLY BROGAN ALIVE AND KICKING!'

GRAVE NEWS FOR 'MARTIANS'.  CURLY BROGAN ALIVE AND KICKING!

A special report by ace reporter - Newsy Parker

Last night in a quiet corner of 'KARS', a Chimeford lounge bar,
I found myself (after having received a mysterious phone
call) sipping Black Russians with a red 'ghost'. Yet only
a few days ago the news of the sudden death of my
drinking companion had stunned the Centaur Car plant.
But here was the man himself, Curly Brogan, as large as
life and twice as gamey!

According to Brogan, his absence had been due to his
attendance at his son's wedding in Torquay, for which the
Company'd granted his unpaid leave. On the eve of the
wedding Brogan had recieved a phone call from his invalid
mother to inform him that a Plod Squad had given his gaff
a real going over. She tried to get out of them what they
were looking for but this cardboard Kojak sticks a
search-warrant under her nose which he claims gives him
the right to dismantle 'this effin commie kennel' down
to the last brick. His claim was endorsed by a uniformed
Plod who was using his batton to rake books from their
shelves in the hope of finding a car engine or a gearbox,
stashed behind a multi-volumd collection entitled: 'The
Rise of Soviet Cummonism.' Lightly slapping his palm
with the truncheon he leans over the complaining old lady
and hisses in'r ear: 'Granny, you'd better hitch a knot
in your whinge-pipe.Coz, if you don't, I'm gonna trash
your cripple-chair and leave you nothing to sit on but
your chuffd.'

Brogan leaned across the table. 'When I catch up with
that sod of a Plod who put the frighteners on Ma, I'm
gonna take his baton and ram it so far up his jaxie he'll
be able to spin his helmet on it.'

Brogan's first impulse was to return home immediately,
but his fiesty old mother vetoed this. It was true the
'nipple heads' had made a helluva mess of the flat, but
at least she'd had the satisfaction of seeingthem leave
empty-handed.

With some reluctance Brogan had accepted his mother's
advice. However, unable to let matters rest he'd later
ducked into a phone kiosk and rang up Frank Jordan. The
distant reciever was lifted, just in time to broadcast a
familiar cough all the way from Chimeford down to Torquay.

'Lo,Frank. Thought I told you to see a vet 'bout that
bark of yours?'

Almost immediately, the line began to deteriorate.

'Frank, give your reciever a rap - see if it'll clear
the static.'

Jordan set about this with so much vigor Brogan was
forced to shout: I said " Rapit" not "zap it!"
'Sthat any better, Curly?'

Jordan's voice sounded as if he was i  a call box on
Pluto.

'Yeah,' Brogan answered. 'Just keep shouting. Come
again?'
'When's the what? The Wedding. It's tomorrow morning.
That's right.Eh? The weather? Diabolical. Pissing
jemmies and javelins...'

At the machine's bidding, Brogan thumbed more coins
into its insatiable slot. 'Listen, Frank' he bawled. 'This
poxy kiosk's running away with all my smash. So drop the
chit-chat. All I want to know'h. why them tit-heads were
crawling all over my flat.'

'Looking for stuff, I suppose.'

'Stuff? What stuff?'

'Stolen stuff.'

'Why'd they think I'd hookey gear in my flat?.'

Jordah's voice was fading fast. 'On account of them
snipes finding them radios i: your locker. I guess.'

'Radios? What radios?'

By then Jordan's speech had dwindled to mere word-
husks, a scattering of vocal chaff. Soon it'd faded .
altogether.

'Frank, you still there?. Can you hear me? Frank...'

The machine's black charge humerals flickered
greedily as  it continued with it's wireway robbery.
Brogan fumbled his replacal of the reciever. It plunged
to hang bouncily on the the whoring black plastic cord. He
chose to leave it there. It presented a visual analogy of
something he didn't want to analyse, not for the present
anyway   ...  '  'Thought you'd taken damned root in
there!' snapped the Blue Rinse who'd been laying seige to
the kiosk with frowns and scowls almost from the moment
Brogan had beaten'r to occupation of it.

'It's out of order, Missus,' said Brogan, ceding to
her possession of the kiosk with its steemy windows and
rain-studded roof. Pausing to zip up his windcheater,
Brogan, with a measure orf disinterest - rather like some
-one in a petshop peering in at the dying convulsions of a
goldfish in a grossly polluted tank - the Blue Rinse's
equally frantic efforts to claw open the kiosk door.
Brogan was amazed to see that're plumpish face was
assmuing a woadlike sheen that would soon make a perfect
match for her blue-rinsed hair.

He nodded. There was no doubt in his mind that those
uncouth scoundrels who'd the malice aforethought to let
loose a horrehdous series of farts moments before they
quit public telephone kiosks, were, as he'd remarked to
the now slowly expiring Pictish lady - well out of order!

# The
# Fade

McQuirr, scarcely half-awake, trudged to the clock-ing-on point. Once there, a yawn froze in his mouth. The Tardis had vanished! The chunky oak and brass machine had been ousted by a newcomer, a computer-ised whippet with a nasty slit of a mouth and luminous red numerals dancing like madness on its brow.

'Stick it in there,' Fawcett, the seats section grey-back, ordered.

McQuirr stared at him.

'Your card.' Fawcett was pointing to the machine's slot.

McQuirr searched the rackful of unfamiliar cards. The greyback frowned. 'Forgotten our number, have we?'

'Two thousand and one!'

'You were issued with a new one – remember?'

McQuirr shook his head.

'In your pay-packet, last week.'

Fawcett's forefinger riffled down the shiny tabs. An irate queue of ops had formed behind McQuirr.

'Does it dish out fivers?' one of them asked

'Be "late-warnings" unless that dozy bastard gets a jildy on,' shouted another.

The greyback located McQuirr's card. He handed it to'm. 'Get on with it!'

McQuirr fumbled the operation and the machine began immediately to bristle with warning lights before finally playing its 'VOID!' card.

Fawcett groaned. 'You've got it arse-for-elb . . . That's better!'

The new time-machine gave an electronic burp and the card popped up.

Tommy Farr, the section shoppy, stopped McQuirr as he trudged towards the seats-hoist. 'Don't forget, there'll be an IE in your section today, John,' Farr warned. 'So, no buckshee breaks, no getting ahead of the game. You know the score. Anyway, Glover'll keep you right.'

'These clock numbers,' McQuirr said.

'What about'm?'

'Look at it,' he grumbled, waving a scrap of paper. (Fawcett'd made McQuirr take note of his new number.) 'Like a machine-part number, How'd the union let'm away with it? Shower of diddies. Organisers? They couldn't organise a piss-up'n a brothel.'

'Brewery, John.'

'What?'

'It's a piss-up'n – never mind. Just remember, soon

as you drop that bit of plastic your name lights up'n five places. Don't be on the "late" print-out, that's all.'

The industrial engineer, Austin Seymour, had settled himself near a stack of seat-frames. Equipped with stopwatch, a selection of coloured pens, clipboard, and time-sheets, he beadily observed the operations taking place in the seats-build area. McQuirr glowered at'm. A locust, that's what he was, sitting there on a twig munching minutes.

'Wish I'd stuck in at borstal,' McQuirr said.

'So's you could be a wank wi' a watch, eh?'

'As long as my bloody arm.'

'Eh?'

'New clock number.'

Glover shook his head. 'You still bitching about that – ?'

'Diabolical, so it is.'

'Slow down a bit,' Glover cautioned, 'that bugger's getting excited.'

McQuirr stacked polythene-wrapped seats alongside others on the floor. He hauled a Sultan rear seat from the unwrapped pile.

'Years, I had that number. Years. That's how I got my nickname.'

'Nickname?'

'Sputnik.'

'What-nik?'

McQuirr cut open a bag and tipped a slithering mass of polythene covers onto the bench. 'After yon Arthur C. Clarke movie: "2001" – remember?

Glover checked off a sequence number on the telex

157

print-out sheet. 'Never heard anybody call you "Sputnik" before.'

'It sort of faded away.' McQuirr took an armful of covers and folded them neatly over the stretched rope. 'It was when I worked on the wet-deck. The lads got to hear my clock number, and – bingo, I'd a nickname!'

'They called you Bingo, did they?'

'No, I told you – "Sputnik".'

'Bingo suits you better,' said the grinning Glover. 'Seeing's you haven't got a full house upstairs.'

'Bugger off!' McQuirr grunted.

During the break McQuirr waylaid 'Gentleman' Jim Corbett as he was passing the snack area. With his neatly-clipped moustache and his impeccably-groomed grey hair he looked like a debonair con man.

'Thought you'd be redundant,' McQuirr said.

Corbett removed his blue-tinted glasses. (For some reason he couldn't speak with them on.) 'Never been busier,' he said. 'Haven't a minute.'

A timekeeper without a minute!

Corbett began to edge around McQuirr. 'Well, must press on.'

'Listen, Jim, do's a favour.'

Alarm spread in Corbett's grey eyes. When a punter wanted a favour it usually involved time or money. The glasses, already halfway to his nose, paused. 'A favour?'

McQuirr nodded, then, dropping his gaze, mumbled something.

'What's that?' Corbett bent closer to catch the words.

McQuirr cleared his throat. 'I was, well, you know, kinda wondering who'd got two thousand and one . . .'

'Two thousand and one what?'

'It's my old clock number. I was just curious who had it.'

'Why?'

'Daft, I know, but –' McQuirr drew Corbett to one side as a forky laden with seat-springs honked past.

'Nobody has it,' Corbett told'm. 'It's gone to that Big Time-Office in the Sky.'

'You sure about that?'

Corbett nodded. 'New system: Plant's been zoned off so that each zone has a max of 300 ops.' He began to explain the ramifications of the introduced system but McQuirr had stopped listening. The timekeeper's glasses slipped over his eyes, then he was off. McQuirr watched him disappearing into the murk of Zombieland, where a welding operation was lobbing lucid blue sparks into the air.

Like a probe, Seymour's penpoint sank into each squandered minute, extracted its essence, then wrote its epitaph in brisk fashion on the time-sheets. The industrial engineer seldom smiled, nor did he allow his scrutiny to wander far from its given task – to locate parasitic growths in the human energy fields: the wasted moment; the extra step; the blight of bad co-ordination; every input of misused muscle power; anything at all which checked or baulked the surging gallop of the Centaur Car Company.

McQuirr sheathed seats, stacked them, marked them off on the sequence sheet, barrowed them across to the hoist. The IE, he suspected, was paying particular attention to him; he could feel his gaze following his every movement as he juggled the three essential elements of his exercise – time, motion, and pause.

Seymour seemed to be relishing the complexity of the equation he was so precisely developing so that the consequences of McQuirr's removal could be gauged. McQuirr sped another surly glance towards the IE. There was no doubting what the twat in the tweed sports jacket was there for – quite simply it was to figure the means of his elimination. This wasn't the first time the Company'd tried to get shot of him. There'd been other 'hangman's rehearsals', as McQuirr called them – a description which brought to mind a movie he'd once seen in which the public hangman had peered through the Judas of the condemned man's cell to determine the prisoner's 'dropistics' – a term the urbane executioner had used, accompanied by a gallows grin. Although less covert about it, the IE was similarly assessing McQuirr.

A trapdoor, its bolts well-oiled with use, dropped open in McQuirr's mind, plunging him once more into the void of 'that bitch of a morning' as he'd tagged it, the one when he'd returned home to find a letter awaiting him. It'd been sent to'm by the Company.

In a few terse lines it thanked him for his job application but regretted its inability at this time to grant him employment at Centaur . . . For McQuirr, who'd been working at the plant for over a decade, this was mind-bending news. His wife had chosen to see the comical side of the screw-up. 'My, my,' she'd laughed, 'you must be really important down there – ten years, and they don't even know you're around!' McQuirr had found nothing laughworthy in the event.

In fact, he'd taken it to be not only an insult but also a warning. Just like the movie's public executioner going through the grisly preliminaries of his profession, using a sandbag as a substitute for the real thing, so the Centaur (the farcical letter'd had been but one of its ploys) measured McQuirr for the drop.

He'd never forget the hour he'd endured trawling the wet streets in search of an unvandalised phonebox. Even yet he remembered the odd sensation he'd had of being adrift from his body, of having to break into a run to catch up with it, for the further he'd got separated from it, the more he'd seemed to vaporise, to become nothing but a trick of light. People – how enviably solid they'd looked! – had seemed to pass through the evaporating cloud-man he'd become. Panic, like pronged lightning, had speared him to the core as his body had given its harried phantom the slip at a pedestrian crossing. Luckily he'd seen his flesh'n bone twin go into a laundrette, where he'd managed to pounce on the wayward body and inveigle himself back into it. A bizarre experience it'd been, one he'd divulged to no one, not even his wife. It was the stuff madness was made from. There was a public phone in the laundrette. While he'd watched a grey shirt having soapy convulsions behind a machine's glass porthole, his identity had been restored. An administrative cock-up, that's all it'd been. He'd accepted the apology but, nevertheless, the obsession had continued to haunt him that the Centaur Car Company was still intent on striking him from its payroll.

Glover nudged McQuirr. 'C'mon for chrissake, John – you're miles away!'

Snapped from his reverie, McQuirr realised that he'd been staring into space, his hands idle. For how long he'd been in this trance he wasn't sure. But Seymour would know; that voracious locust feasted on every unproductive moment, sucked it dry.

McQuirr's hands writhed in the slippery polythene, sought to grapple with its slick nothingness. He drew envelope after transparent envelope over velour-trimmed seats, and the more he dealt with, piling them up to his left, the more seats streamed off the carousel. His movements were jerky, uncoordinated. Quite often the polythene wrapper split and he'd to rip it off, junk it. From the corner of his eye he caught Glover's puzzled-looking glances. He was probably trying to work out whether he was putting on an act for the IE or was genuinely uptight about something. Was he ever anything else but uptight these days? The other night, for instance, while watching TV, the image of a fissuring iceberg had sent him panicking from his armchair. His alarmed wife reckoned it was high time he visited a head-doctor.

But the Centaur Car Company didn't employ an industrial psychologist. When faced with the mental casualties that came off-track with their cars, the Company tended to rely upon the 'it-never-happened' strategy. So, should a disturbed operator sit down one day by the edge of the flowing track and give way to an unrestrainable fit of sobbing, or if a cackling greyback in the canteen took the notion to fill his shoes with custard, the remedy was to deny it'd ever occurred. With a blanket of secrecy thrown over him, the unfortunate 'breakdown' would be taken to the edge of some administrative ravine and hurled over. Now and again the wan phantom of a victim might be seen wandering in its old working area but inevitably it would fade away. McQuirr, Glover, and a chaser called Troy usually did the crossword during the lunchbreak. But not today, it seemed. Rising suddenly to his feet, as if reacting to the clue Troy'd just read out – 'Has this Wellsian character been overdoing the vanishing cream? (3,9,3)' – McQuirr jettisoned the remaining tea from his mug, making a black star on the concrete floor.

'Where're you off to?' asked Glover.

'Breath of air.'

'It's pissing out there, man!'

McQuirr shrugged his shoulders. As he walked away, he overheard Glover say: 'If you ask me – the bugger's cracking up!'

As if the rain wasn't flooding the yard fast enough, the wind was cuffing water over the storage tank's rim. McQuirr stood near the half-shut doors of the loading bay. He watched the water's white leaping, saw it cascading down the sides of the tank. It was in that black funnel that Alf Sheridan had done away with himself. Yeah, he'd climbed the ladder and, dressed in chains, had taken the freedom-plunge. He hadn't so much as scribbled a line to explain his bizarre exit. It was generally accepted though that the sudden death of his wife had triggered his actions. Grief was the planet's deadliest and most-to-be-feared poison: compared to its slow, agonising effects the mamba with its sudden black lightning was a mercy-killer.

McQuirr went into the body'n white section and

163

paused between lines of raw, unpainted Sultan saloons, the metal blemishes of which had been blue-circled for the discers. A roof leak tapped out a tattoo on an empty paint drum. From the snack areas came the low rumble of men's voices and the occasional yelps of triumph from card winners. Some of these ops turned in their seats to rake McQuirr with suspicious stares. Conscious of their scrutiny, he felt a bit foolish as he pawed his way down a rackful of glossy new time-cards. It seemed that Corbett hadn't been having him on, after all: there was no card to be found with a higher numerical value than 300.

'You there! Where's your permit?'

The question was volleyed from behind a group of Sultan Estate shells. Stricken motionless by it, McQuirr suddenly relaxed. 'Jeez, Biggles, you scared me shitless there!'

Biggles Blane, the Sequencer, emerged from the shells. He approached McQuirr with fists raised and did a bit of mock-sparring. 'How goes it, Sputnik, me old son?' He dropped his hands. 'What're you arsing around here for?' He mimed a casting motion with an invisible fishing rod. 'You still drowning worms?'

'Had to get shot of my gear,' McQuirr told'm. 'Rheumatics.'

Biggles' grin widened. 'Don't come the fanny. You've already used that one to work your ticket from the wet-deck.' They walked on together. 'You should see the rod I'm packing now,' Biggles said. 'A right cracker. Telling you, take out a pike like it was a sardine.' This was the prelude to a fishy tale that kept Biggles' mouth busy until they'd reached the main door of the stores area. They looked out at the rain. Biggles nodded in the direction of the nearby Broadmoor.

'Fancy a squint at your redundancy?'

McQuirr frowned. 'Redundancy?'

'Yeah. Them Daleks. Bastards'll weld anything that moves. C'mon, let's have a shufty.'

Battered by the rain, they skirted around puddles and dripping pallet stacks and went into Broadmoor. A group of ops stood in the area where the unimates had been installed. In all there were twenty-two of these robot welders, eleven to each side of the track. McQuirr eyed one. It looked more like a praying mantis than a Dalek, standing there with beaky head poised, awaiting the power that would have it pecking out welds at a rate no human could hope to match. An engineer who'd apparently elected himself as tour-guide was rapping out impressive stats: 'They can handle over one hundred car-shells an hour.' He reached to finger the skeletal neck of the unimate nearest to'm. 'For that level of output you'd require over two hundred operatives . . .'

A grey-haired op who stood near McQuirr said, 'You should see'm when they get going: like hens in a byre midden!'

McQuirr and Biggles walked around the machines, squinting at them from different angles. 'Soon won't need us, eh?' said Biggles. He shrugged. 'I guess we're for the broth pot.'

Maybe it was this remark or perhaps the sight of those brutish muzzles poised, waiting, that'd sent the pellets of dread skittering down the slope of McQuirr's mind. There was no restraining them as they gathered velocity, prising loose old fears as well as an avalanche of new anxieties.

'Give you the creeps, eh?' Biggles went on, completely unaware that he was speaking to a phantom which despite desperate resistance was being slowly ejected from its body. 'A lick of oil'nd a tap'n the arse with a spanner, that's all they need. Never strike, never shit, and never get hangovers.'

Back'n the body'n white, they passed swiftly amongst the crates and pallets of metal stampings, and skirted puddles in which dull rainbows glimmered. McQuirr's runaway body was now well clear of its former occupant. It capered around, waving its arms and looking slyly about itself; clearly, it was plotting mischief. Biggles Blane, still oblivious of the bewildered spook at his elbow, dropped out when a punter from the plant's angling club stopped him for a bit crack.

Meanwhile, McQuirr's body had brought a painter's ladder crashing to the concrete floor before it began to hurl door hinges up at the complaining tradesman, who quickly ducked for cover amongst the roof girders. McQuirr's body now sent a forky driver tumbling from his seat and commandeered the vehicle itself. With its rightful driver shouting in pursuit it charged the rubber doors that led to the paintshop, where it was afforded not only the props to make mischief on an unprecedented scale but also to make it in glorious colour!

McQuirr, who'd given up all hope of reconnection with his body, wandered around the plant. He felt himself fading, becoming progressively drained of energy, so much so that soon he was looking for a corner in which to hide himself. But everywhere he turned he found a clone of Austin Seymour, complete with stopwatch, pens, clipboard, and time-sheets, waiting for him. Such obscenities plagued the place, breeding, hatching out. Those things in Broadmoor with their fiery beaks and their staunchless energies would multiply too. Able to outweld two hundred men, from them would come a flux of inhuman power that, like a bore tide, would surge up the metal rivers that ran throughout the plant, and all the hourly-paid minnows who swam in those streams would be swept away.

Officially, the incident in which McQuirr was involved that afternoon never happened. The personnel records might show, 'Dismissed due to industrial misconduct' or, more accurately, 'Discharged for medical reasons', but the details of what actually 'never happened' remain oral. Since Glover was McQuirr's working partner, his version of what really took place was judged to be nearest the mark:

'Well, as I said, he'd been jumpy all morning. It was obvious after chuck time that he'd been out'n the rain. I mean any daft bugger who'd go out in the piss when he didn't have to, well, he's got t'be one short of the full deck – right? So, he starts going on about them auto-welders they've stuck'n Broadmoor, only he calls 'em Daleks. They were going to take over, that's all he kept saying. Nothing the unions could do 'bout stopping 'em – that kinda shit. To listen to'm you would've thought they was out t'have his job in particular.

'Any roads, he clams up for a bit. Done that a lot, McQuirr. One minute it's gab-gab, the next it's the "broodies". Y'know, go into trances, stare into space. Gave me the creeps it did. Well, it happened this way: Seymour, who's doing the watch number on us, slopes off for a riddlemeree or something. Leaves his clipboard'n time-sheets on a crate, don't he? And that's when it happened. It was like something went twang inside McQuirr's noggin. Next I knows, don't he go rushing across to where Seymour's sheets are, lifts the whole batch and, before you could blink, he's made confetti of it! But he's not finished. He grabs a can from the glue table and scampers with it towards the new time-puncher. But the loopy bugger'd gone'nd lumbered himself with a duff can that should've been binned on account of its glue having hardened off. He could've stood there till kingdom come waiting for a pour.

'Clueless, as well as glueless now, he takes to bashing the time-puncher with the can. Brained the bloody thing. Put its lights out. By then, of course, the Bull comes charging from his office and sticks an arm-lock on McQuirr, What's that? Took a swing at the Bull? No way. That's crap! I'll tell you what the poor sap did – began to blub, that's what. Pathetic.

'They took'm into the office but couldn't get tuppence-worth of sense out of'm. All the time he keeps parroting his clock number, his old one, that is – 2001. Eh? Come back here? No chance! By the time he gets out of the booby-hatch he'll be on two wheels and zombie's zube-zubes. Come again? Miss'm? I suppose so. He could be a bit of diddy at times but he was quite good at crosswords . . .'

## BREATHALISER TESTS  FOR HIGH)TRACK OPS?

On Friday last there was hearly a nasty accident in MAD
when one of the so-called "Younmg Torques"'; Errol Gray,
was seen to be clearly under the influence of canteen
tea and to be operating his torque-wrench in a meanner
so wreckless that he seemed likely to endangr the sleep
of those ops in his vicinity.The traffic-snipes mounted a
suveillance of Gray which revealed : (1) that the torquer
freuently tightened his assigned bolts at an excessive
speed; (2) that, weaving erraticakly and overspeeding
he made lewd hand-signals at his greybacks, not to mentian
his singing filthy ditties that female ops complained
were disgusting in the extreme; (3) a radar trap clocked
Gray to be doing well over the ton during a line- stoppagge
whiich took'm seven stations out-of-place.

When arrested by the traffic - snipes, Errol "Gray,
was described as being "in a fuddled state, and that he
kept saying: " Wheresh the blurry swish for swishing
ωΩℓ thiℓ bluriy ming!"

A breathaliser-test revealed that the torque-op had drunk
in excess of 9 mugs of canteen char - which accounts for
his reprenhensible state.

This incident will probably lead to the random
breathalising of MAD ops in order to trap ton-up tea-hog
types. Said Centaur Traffic Chief, Nathan Dulanski.
" We are determined to stamp out this menace!""

So saying, Dulanski leapt onto his customised tea
trolley, and, giving its accelerator welly, scorched off
like a maniac.

### LEND ME YOUR EARS – ALL TWO OF THEM!

The scrapping of the mono-lug muffler and its replacal
with the bi-lug version, seems, to judge from the plant
op's total apathy, to've fallen on deaf ears!
A " Broadmoor" op was seemingly amazed to learn that
he had in fact two ears; apparently he'd been usng his "spare"
one as an ashtraay!


### HIGH DRAMA ON THE HIGH TRACK

The news is that Centaur, Chimeford's H$^U$cus-Pocus
Film Club has at last completed their long-awaited movie:
.Horror on the Hightrack!" It stars some of the residents
from the country's top lunaitic asylums, who are expexted
to get rave reports for their gritty depiction of life in a
modern car factory.
The film world awaits the Premier with mounting excitement.

# Twitcher
# Haskins
# Gets
# the Bird!

Mail trickled onto the hall floor, then the letterbox snapped shut. Simultaneously, the toaster ejected underdone slices from its wan fire, and lapsed into darkness. Haskins reset the machine, and with geriatric grumblings its element regrouped its feeble energies. He glanced into the pan on the stove. The pair of eggs joggling in the boiling water had cracked, and the timer, having all but emptied its upper chamber, was on the point of obsoleting itself. Haskins filled, then plugged in the kettle, and was moving hallwards to fetch the mail when Dora, with a gruff-voiced, 'I'll get it,' wheeled past the kitchen doorway. Soon Haskins heard the pecking sound of Dora's lifting device (her 'third arm' she called it) as it dipped to snap up postal items in its aluminium jaws then, with an upward tossing motion, flicked them onto her lap. Meanwhile, the kitchen wall-clock had begun its eight o'clock kerfuffle: first, a wing-whirring sound; next, a loud crack like Time itself fracturing; following this came the cuckoo's frantic beak-rapping on the inner side of the clock's unyielding door.

Something burning!

In three strides, so swiftly taken that his leg joints crackled in protest, Haskins reached the toaster and rammed up its power lever. Some moments later Dora propelled her chair into the smoke-hazed kitchen. Haskins, scraping burnt toast at the sink, glanced over his shoulder. With her third arm clamped sceptre-like across her chest she looked a dead ringer for old Queen Victoria in one of her grumpy moods. The carriage rolled into Dora's customary place at the table; its powerpack's dusky whine had scarcely died away before its occupant's began:

'What's burning?'

'My shirt-tail – what d'you think?'

'How you managed to burn anything on that heap of scrap's beyond me.' She began to gather the mail from her lap. 'I don't suppose there's any chance of them presenting you with a toaster today?' She wagged her grey head. 'No such luck. It'll probably be something completely useless, like a clock.'

Haskins shook his head. 'It's not always clocks. Frank Moolens got golf clubs, and Tony Larscombe a deluxe chess set when they retired.'

She nodded. 'As I said – completely useless. By the way, George, I trust you're not counting on getting something "deluxe".'

'Why shouldn't I?'

'Well, let's face it, they haven't exactly pushed the boat out for you, have they? I mean, twelve noon in the old personnel office! Why don't they hold the damned thing in the car park'nd be done with it?'

Haskins frowned. 'We've been through all that. Anyway. I hardly see that my presentation concerns you since you've made it abundantly clear that you've no intention of attending it.'

'That wasn't called for, George.' Her voice sounded wobbly. 'I've hit a bad patch. You know that. I'm simply not up to it.'

He nodded. 'Sorry.'

'The kettle's boiling,' she told'm.

'So it is. Lucky you're here. Might not've spotted it.'

'Don't be sarky.' Her brow puckered. 'I do wish you'd have done with that. Irritates me it does – all that skrepp-skrepping.'

'Maybe I should go out to the garage.'

From the corner of his eye Haskins saw her third arm rising to indicate the **pan** on the cooker. Silently, he began to count to ten.

'Those eggs sound cracked,' said Dora.

'They're not alone.'

'What's that?'

'Nothing, dear.' He cleared his throat, then in a sort of jollying-up tone, one completely alien to'm, he asked her what was in the mail. 'Stacks of best-wishes cards for the retiree, eh?'

'There's just the one,' she said. 'That'nd a telly-licence reminder, your bird thingy, and a letter from Pearl.' Her tone altered. 'I take it the eggs are cracked?'

175

Haskins nodded. 'I'll mash'm in a cup with some butter.'

'Burnt toast'nd cracked eggs – some breakfast!' She shook her head! 'I wish to God I'd the power of my legs. I – '

' – wouldn't see you in my road!' Haskins silently mouthed her familiar plaint. A cobwebbed sitcom, that's what their marriage had become: 'The George'nd Dora Show!' Depression, like the carbon shadow in the sink, began to darken his thoughts, becoming blacker still with each scrape of her carping tongue.

As if this wasn't bad enough, a luminous worm had begun to wriggle at the inner corner of his left eye, an optical disturbance that signalled the onset of one of his migraine attacks. Soon, the glow-worm would reproduce a clone of itself in his other eye, and the dazzling duplicates would then, displaying equally corrosive appetites, begin to gnaw holes in his vision.

Haskins placed a freshly-scraped toast portion on a plate then, sighing, he reached for the remaining charred slice. This was it! This was them for the rest of their lives, a pair of juiceless old fossils buried in a graveyard of dead hopes. Trapped, they were, just like the cuckoo in its Swiss jail. Doing time together, without hope of remission. Relentlessly, Haskins went on with the skrepp-skrepping.

But he needn't have bothered: Dora, having rejected what was on offer, settled instead for brown bread with a light smearing of honey. Her preparation of this, without resort to scowls, sighs, or sarcasm, seemed, as far as Haskins could judge, to signal an end to breakfast hostilities.

Sitting opposite her while she read her sister's letter, Haskins flicked through the pages of his magazines, mainly glancing at the pictures, for the optical light-flickerings had intensified, so much so that it made reading too difficult for'm.

How he relished exotic bird names: the Pallid Swift, Ivory Gull, Sociable Plover, Black Kite, Dark Chanting Goshawk . . . These days, though, his magazine was proving to be more of a torment than a pleasure. As Dora's condition worsened, so the range of his birding activities had correspondingly shrunk, until he'd had to make do with the meagre specimens available to'm in local haunts.

If this encroachment on his favourite pastime continued – and, given the nature of Dora's illness, it would – he'd soon become a 'couch-twitcher', staring glumly into his tiny garden or listlessly watching grossly over-edited bird programmes on the telly, maybe even stooping to sending off pathetic letters to the editors of 'tick-hunting' mags: 'Dear Ed, just shooting you a line to let you know that a Blunt-Beaked Swiss Cuckoo has taken up residence in my kitchen clock . . .'

Dora said something. Haskins glanced up from his magazine. 'Sorry?'

She indicated her letter. 'Pearl wants to drop by for a holiday – a couple of weeks or so. She's obviously not gotten over Michael yet, poor dear. Be nice having her. Ages since I've seen'r in the flesh. Why, I do believe it's as long ago as the funeral. Make a pleasant change having her here. Different conversation.' She frowned. 'In fact, any conversation – even one with a lock-jawed parrot – would be a rarity in this house.' She released such a deep sigh, it seemed she must've gone to the very bottom of her soul for it. 'God only knows what it'll be like having you under my wheels all day!'

Haskins had begun some finger-play with the envelope which presumably contained good wishes from someone on the occasion of his retirement. From across the table he could sense a storm brewing, a verbal tornado fuelling itself with feminine curiosity. He teased it along a little by replacing the envelope on the table then, like a Braille reader, grazed the tip of his index finger to'nd fro across his name and address.

Hurricane Dora finally struck! 'Why don't you stop fiddling with that envelope and open the damned thing?'

He smiled, then, with a shoulder shrug, said, 'Just savouring the novelty of it, that's all.'

She nodded. 'As you sow, so shall you reap.'

Dora began to refold Pearl's letter, her contorted fingers labouring along its creases, closing it down. Meanwhile, her sermon continued: 'Friendships aren't like apples on a tree, George. You can't simply reach up'n pluck one down when the notion takes you. Friendships have to be worked at – cultivated.'

'Or dispensed with entirely,' said Haskins. 'In my line of work, "pals" were liabilities. If they got into a fix they expected you to lie'nd cover up for them!' Haskins lifted the envelope. 'That's why, you see, I didn't "cultivate" friends, why I chose to be a man apart.'

'For goodness sake, George, you were a factory flatfoot – not a Trappist monk!'

Haskins ripped open the envelope.

The first thing to hook his attention was the drawing on the front of the card: – it depicted a man-eating magpie. The wretch writhing in its ferocious beak – he wore a Nazi uniform – was a caricature of Haskins, himself.

The magpie was straddling a colossal nest that brimmed with auto parts: wheels, tyres, car bonnets, headlamps, batteries, radios, alternators, etc. Inside the card, in bold lettering, a sardonic greeting caught his glance.

HERE'S WISHING
TWITCHER HASKINS
A VERY SHORT
RETIREMENT

Beneath this, in rolling blue handwriting, there appeared a verse:

> You sought'm here,
> You sought'm there,
> You sought that Magpie
> Everywhere.
> Was he in Broadmoor?
> Or maybe in MAD?
> Now you'll never know,
> Ain't that too bad!
> Never mind, Twitcher,
> This card's to remind you
> That your future is brief
> And your present's behind you!

179

In low spirits, nearing high noon, Haskins drove his Warlord Red Sultan Super the fifteen miles or so between his bungalow and the Centaur Car Plant. Several times during the short journey he'd been tempted to turn back; an immense expanding rivet of pain seemed to be in the process of embedding itself deeper'nd deeper into his skull. He mopped his brow with a hankie. All this hassle for a clock! Why couldn't companies reward long and faithful service with something more imaginative, like tickets for a world cruise, as someone had suggested the other day on the radio? Snags abounded though, health and fitness being prime factors.

Anyway, he hated travelling and found exotic sun-traps to be just that – traps! A clock, though, did seem a daft thing to be dishing out in recognition of a working lifetime. He had to admit it, Dora was right. But what could you do? Hand it back, saying, 'I'd rather you paid off my mortgage, please.' Haskins sighed. Absurd or not he'd just have to go through with it. Life seemed to have this habit of forcing you to comply with its ludicrous and often petty demands. Once again, like a diverted river creeping back to its old workings, its familiar runs, his mind returned to the item of hate-mail he'd received that morning. Certainly, he was well used to being the target of brickbats. In his long and lonely journey to become Supersnipe, he'd been dubbed with malicious nicknames like Sergeant Stench, Eichmann, and, of course, the soubriquet that'd really stuck: The Twitcher!

That the poison card had upset Dora had been plain to see.

'What a vile mind he must have,' she'd said with a disgusted headshake as she'd flung The Magpie's malicious card onto the table. 'Imagine concocting, never mind posting, such filth!'

'Could've been worse, I suppose,' said Haskins, 'a letter-bomb, maybe.'

'You must report it, George. He's obviously deranged. That stuff about "a short retirement" – a threat, that's what it amounts to.' She'd glared at'm across the table. 'You can wag your head till it rolls off, mister. But, mark my words, some maniac's out to get you! Phone and tell'm you can't make it. Say I'm ill (which isn't a lie), tell'm the house is on fire or that you've been knocked groggy by one of your migraines –'

He grimaced, 'That wouldn't be a lie either, believe me.' Haskins raised a hand to his pain-cudgelled skull. 'I've got the mother'nd father of all headaches. Been fisting over painkillers like they were Smarties.'

She nodded in sympathy. 'You do look an awful colour, George. D'you want me to phone them?' Gratified by her obvious concern for his well-being, he nevertheless shook his head. 'I must go, Dora. People've gone to a lot of bother on my behalf.'

With a report loud enough to make Haskins jump and to jolt tears of pain into her eyes, Dora brought her palm down with a resounding smack on the table. 'People!' she'd bawled. 'I'll give you people!'

The Magpie'd become a legendary figure in the Centaur Car plant. The operators relished hearing about the audacious ploys (some true – most fanciful) by which he continually outsmarted the snipes. Every store audit which revealed 'deficiencies due to theft' Haskins took to be a personal insult, a challenge to his efficiency, a fact which KIKBAK played up with its usual vigorous mockery: 'THE GREAT GLOVE GRAB', for instance, had fairly bristled with sarcasm:

'The Magpie sure flung the gauntlet at the flat feet of the snipes when he made off with a handy haul of industrial gloves – around one thousand pairs, at the last finger-count! Twitcher Haskins who, as we know, is to security what Ghengis Khan was to ballroom dancing, nearly had mittens, sorry, kittens, when told of The Magpie's latest exploit. He promised, yet again, "to leave no stone upturned in his unflagging efforts to unmask this pernicious industrial Fagan".

'Sounds to us, chums, not only like a busted metaphor, but also the usual Mag-pie-in-the-sky rhetoric that's to be heard dribbling with increasing frequency from his senile lips. It's just as well that he'll soon be hanging up his jackboots. He plans to spend his retirement breeding edible Japanese slugs and he also plans to cultivate a new variety of poison ivy. By the way, your Slugship, remember to wear gloves when you're handling these plants since contact with your skin could prove fatal – for the ivy!

'Now, don't hesitate to ring us if you need gloves for your barbecues. We can supply them at prices that are finger-pricking good. Don't forget – y'hear!'

Catching The Magpie was, of course, always going to be the tough bit. For starters, where was he based? Haskins figured it had to be in MAD because that was where most spares were stored. He'd ruled out the likelihood of the thief being either a high-track or sub-assembly op – the former because such workers were too tightly tethered to The Widow, and although the subbies enjoyed greater mobility, it was Haskins' opinion that they were too exposed to mount such an extensive and clandestine operation.

It was only after two weeks of pondering the matter that it'd dawned on Haskins that he'd been guilty of mind-set. The Magpie didn't have to be an hourly-paid op – he could just as easily be a staff member! This option immediately opened a whole new wedge of possibilities. According to the criteria formulated by Haskins, The Magpie, in order to carry out his criminal activities, would have to enjoy: (i) mobility; (ii) knowledge of spare parts' locations; (iii) frequent visits to the high track; (iv) familiarity with The Widow's greybacks and ops; (v) and – a crucial necessity – ability to come'nd go between sections with his clipboard and order sheets. That there turned out to be a staff grade that ably met these requirements, namely the stockchasers, was an outcome which produced short-term elation for the Supersnipe, for, in the end, his speculation proved to be merely academic. Before he could implement covert surveillance of the MAD stockchasers, he'd been branded with that most dreaded of prefixes – Ex. From yesterday, as it happened, he'd become an ex-Centaur employee, an ex-salary earner, an ex-Supersnipe, and in just a few minutes from now he'd be for the last time in the company of his ex-colleagues.

Tom Jowett and Paul Peakham were the officers on duty at the plant's southside gatehouse. Haskins drove from the slip-road and stopped his car just short of the barrier-pole. Like a newly retired sheriff sensing for the first time the burden of his empty gun holster, Haskins sounded an almost timid horn toot. At the same time he force-fed an ingratiating smile onto his usually mirthless lips. This novel show of deference was down to his recognition that the gatehouse duo were no longer his inferiors. In fact, although they were merely a raw pair of padlock-pullers, they out-aced their former boss simply by being on the company's payroll. Technically, they could debar him from using his former exec's auto-slot, could if they chose refuse'm entry and redirect'm to Calamity Corner, a cratered expanse of concrete used for parking by the punters.

To his relief this possible humiliation didn't happen. Certainly, neither officer returned his smile nor showed any sign of friendliness, never mind recognition. Their attitude was one of cold efficiency. Without delay the barrier-pole was raised and he was curtly waved through. His 'friendly' hand salute was not reciprocated. Feeling a bit snubbed, Haskins, for the last time, drove his car into the Centaur plant and parked it amongst the up-market models that belonged to the factory's élite.

As Haskins, with all the eagerness of a man stretching his neck on an execution block, trudged towards the old personnel office, the familiar citron yellow van of Harry Ratzo Runciman, pest controller, came wheel-storming the dust as it bucked the maximum-10-m.p.h. speed-limit within the plant and, with its horn blaring, swept past the startled Haskins. As it did so, the rodent-buster smirked from his cab at the Supersnipe and mimed combing his hair, a jeering reference to Haskins' balding head. The furious ex-security chief was left to slap dust from his clothes and to glare after the departing van, which was still sounding its raucous horn.

Ratzo Runciman was down in Haskins' book as 'unfinished business', as, of course, was The Magpie. The Supersnipe had long suspected that in order to preserve job continuity the pest exterminator occasionally brought live cockroaches, mice'nd rats into the plant, that he was a mobile plague on wheels, the propagator of major infestations. It was too late now for Haskins to take any action. Fate'd denied'm Ratzo's greasy scalp, just as it'd prevented'm from plucking a single feather from the elusive Magpie.

He'd passed his file re the pair of rogues, plus some other outstanding security matters, onto Mark Steeley, who'd been elected as Haskins' successor. If it'd been left to the ex-Supersnipe, Steeley wouldn't've got a sniff at the job. His security work was, in Haskins' opinion, far too sloppy to merit such a prime promotion. He was crucially short on objectivity and lacked that absolute must-have for successful industrial policing – a streak of ruthlessness.

Force of habit had caused Haskins to reach up to give the peak of his hat a tug, an intention thwarted by the fact that he was hatless, an absence which gave'm the peculiar sensation that he was wearing somebody else's head. His 'civvies', too, made'm feel as vulnerable as a turtle peeled from its shell; he'd've much preferred to've worn his uniform but this'd been vetoed by Dora. 'For heavens sake, George, show them you've at least one suit in your wardrobe . . .'

Beth Galton, the presentation's organiser, was waiting to pounce on Haskins as he came through the main doorway. 'Where's your wife, then?' she wanted to know.

' 'Fraid she took one of'r turns this morning – couldn't manage. Sorry.'

She glowered at'm through her intimidating glasses. 'Well,' she said dryly, 'you'll just have to accept the bouquet on her behalf, won't you?'

The thought of standing there in public with a bunch of blooms in one hand and a clock in the other was definitely lacking in appeal to Haskins. Why hadn't he turned back when he'd the chance? Too late now. Taking a deep breath he followed Beth Galton into the obsolete office.

As he came in a shaft of sunlight pierced a mucky window pane, then, suggesting Beth Galton's organising talents extended to solar reaches, the sunbeam culled gleams from the high slope of his balding head and tagged the guest-of-honour's progress across the floor, lending a highly theatrical air to his entrance. A spattering of applause arose from the assembled audience, which in some manner had become synchronised with the sunbeam, so that when it suddenly blinked out like a wonky spotlight, the clapping too immediately ceased.

Haskins was astonished at the turn-out – there were enough people present to've manned three firing squads. It was difficult, though, to estimate just how many of those who were heaping their paper plates with the varied fare on offer at the buffet table, or sampling the wine, were there voluntarily. Not many,

Haskins suspected. Probably, the majority of them had either been 'short-strawed' or dragooned into attendance by their departmental heads. The ex-Supersnipe's ego was given an unexpected boost, though, when Beth Galton led him across to the handshakes of not one Martian but two of them, senior ones at that. Why, Conrad Bunston of the finance division was definitely in the first ten, while Matt Kibbley must rank around fifteenth, although the Rumour Machine predicted that this Martian, because of his screw-up with the SM's Poacher, would soon be going Humpty-Dumpty – in other words, he'd have a great fall down the grades, as low maybe as the staff equivalent of pushing broom in Punterland – management of OPC (Obsolete Parts Control).

Freelance photographer Jerry Sangster often carried out assignments for *Centaur Lines* – surely the most boring in-house magazine in the entire auto-world. In fact the incorrigible KIKBAK had once issued a spoof edition of *Lines* which, amongst other items of teeth-crushing boredom, had included an article entitled: 'Czechoslovakian Grommets: Their History, Design and Efficiency Ratio.' Sangster's Jap snapbox flashed into action as Haskins and the Martians exchanged handshakes.

'C'mon, Mr Kibbley, smiles are for free,' he called aloud. 'Won't cost you a penny. Honest. You too, Mr Haskins, d'you think you could brighten it up a tad. You look more like you're expiring than retiring.'

It was at that moment, while Sangster in a childish, wheedling tone, tried to cajole a smile from Kibbley that the ex-Supersnipe caught a glimpse of the developed outcome of this nonsense: he saw himself about three weeks hence, gawking from an ink-mired page of *Centaur Lines*, an old, balding man in a rumpled suit who, standing between the towering Martians, looked tinier than he was in reality. Bunston, his wine-glass raised in salute to the retiree, had managed to get his lips around a grin; Kibbley continued doing his doleful impression of a man standing on the edge of an abyss watching his dentures go chattering down into its darkness.

Having already used up what seemed to've been around a mile of film, the bedazzled Haskins was dismayed to hear Sangster inviting Mark Steeley to join them.

'C'mon,' he called aloud to'm, 'let's be having that newly-promoted carcass over here.'

Haskins frowned as Steeley came ambling from a group of snipes who'd stationed themselves near the improvised wine-bar and were keeping its attendant, Rose Renwick, a sleepy-eyed girl from personnel, busy. Although quite a lot of people had approached Haskins with handshakes and happy retirement wishes, so far not one solitary snipe had availed himself of the opportunity. Huffy so'n'sos. If they'd stuck to their duties as well as they did to their grudges the plant's security might've been a whole wedge tighter. The snipes' disaffection towards their leader could be traced back to the time when he'd ordered them to muster before'm. Briskly he'd gone down the line-up of snipes and reprimanded virtually the entire squad for sartorial sloppiness, overlong hair, and underdone shoe-polish. Then had come his notorious, hackles-raising remark. 'Right,' he'd bawled, 'I want every officer present who owns a Centaur car to take a step forward.' About a dozen or so puzzled-looking snipes complied. 'These men,' Haskins had shouted, as with a sweep of his hand he'd indicated the Centaur-car owners, 'these men are all potential thieves!' Incensed, the obliquely maligned snipes had promptly walked off the job, and got full support from their non-Centaur-car-owning buddies.

The Centaur Industrial Arbitration services had a trying time of it as they'd sought to bind up the snipes' injured pride, to pour balm on their hurt feelings. But even their velvet-glove treatment hadn't been enough to placate the strikers. Bob Crispens, the snipes' senior shoppy, had indicated that nothing short of an apology from the security chief could resolve the dispute. An outraged Haskins categorically refused to comply with this proposal.

At this stage the snipes' industrial action hadn't hampered car production, although with junior management personnel manning the gates, theft just had to be on the increase.

The ACTSS Convenor, Bill Burrage, called a mass meeting of the union's entire staff force which included the shopfloor grades of stockchasers, cycle-checkers, and sequencers. The ACTSS office grades comprised analysts, schedulers, secretaries, punchcard operators and a miscellany of general office workers. There was little doubt that ACTSS working in combination packed enough industrial muscle to inflict formidable damage to Centaur's production programme. For a staff union that wasn't noted for militancy, to their leader's surprise and the Martians' chagrin, this time the bulk of the union's membership voted in favour of possible strike action, which gave Burrage a strong hand in his subsequent talks with the CIA.

These discussions had soon run into barbed-wire and a major track stoppage loomed. However, before the crunch actually came, Haskins (had a Martian leaned on'm?) backed down and offered a sort of diffused apology: since he, himself, was a Centaur car owner, he admitted it might've been more diplomatic if he'd lined up with those men he'd slurred. He, therefore, accepted that he too was a potential thief, or, since the phrase seemed to offend them, that Centaur owners were more likely to be tempted to pinch the odd spark-plug or whatever. The compromise'd been grudgingly accepted but the snipes had never forgiven him.

By the time the photo-session with Haskins and Steeley was over, the ex-Supersnipe was suffering from severe flashbite, a condition that caused gross maculations to float across his vision, creating the illusion that he was staring into a tankful of tadpoles. A sledge-hammer continued to pound what felt like a massive red-hot rivet deeper into his skull. Meanwhile, the presentation itself drew nearer. Beth Galton had steered Bunston behind the table, and was now urgently signalling for Haskins to join him there. He decided to make'r wait a little. It didn't do to be seen scurrying obediently to her every finger-snap.

'Have you had a look at the dossier yet?' he asked.

Steeley grinned. 'I was about halfway through it before I realised it was a wind-up.'

'What d'you mean – a "wind-up"?'

Steeley's grin persisted. 'That stuff about Ratzo Runciman – a rodent-runner, eh? What a hoot! You really had me going.'

'It wasn't intended as a joke,' Haskins said tetchily.

'C'mon, George. For starters, how'd you go about proving it? Search Ratzo's van everytime he comes into the plant? S'that what you had in mind? "Two shovels of live roaches – in. (Check!) One sack containing fifty rodents – in. (Check!)" ' Steeley shook his head. 'I really thought you were having me on. I mean a pest exterminator bugging his own patch – that's really wild, George. Like something out of KIKBAK. I couldn't stop laughing. "What d'you know,' I said to myself, "old Sobersides has a sense of humour, after all!" Then didn't you go'n spoil things by coming that shit about The Magpie?'

Only just keeping his temper in check, Haskins said, 'I was forgetting, you don't even believe he exists, do you?'

Shaking his head, Steeley responded, 'He exists the way Robin Hood exists – as a legend. There's no flesh'n blood reality, no MAD stockchaser and his band of merry men.'

There were several calls of 'You're wanted!' from people standing close to Haskins. From the corner of his eye he could see a livid-faced Beth Galton bearing down on him.

'Your Sheriff of Nottingham had the same flaw as yourself, George,' said Steeley.

'And what might that be?'

'He couldn't see the hoods for the trees either.'

A heavy hand fell upon Haskins' shoulder. 'Yes, yes,' he said, 'I'm coming!'

'Good. Let's hope you mean today,' said Beth Galton.

The presentation, once it was under way, went off with surprising ease. Conrad Bunston told a few droll stories, and, since it was a security man who was retiring, he risked the hoary anecdote about the guy who left the factory every day with a barrowload of topsoil. The gate-cops stopped'm, of course, to make sure he wasn't concealing anything under the dirt, which he never was. This goes on every day for about a month, the same guy at the same time with his barrowload of soil. It's only when the annual audit comes around that plant security discover that over thirty brand-new wheelbarrows've been stolen!

Although most of the audience, which was now deserting the delights of the buffet, not to mention the wine-bar, had probably already heard the Martian's joke they, nevertheless, accorded it some polite titters as they began to congregate around the presentation table. But they seemed to genuinely relish the spectacle of the former security primo's vivid blush as Rose Renwick, stiffling a yawn, presented him with a floral bouquet on behalf of his absent wife, Dora. He was within milliseconds of having the wretched moment recorded for posterity, but, just in time, he spotted Sangster's black camera, like a shark's dorsal fin cleaving its way through the crowd in his direction and he quickly jettisoned the crackling cellophaned package onto the table.

Beth Galton now approached, bearing the presentation itself. She placed the package before the smiling Conrad Bunston, then withdrew. Bunston got to his feet then, nodding towards the paper-wrapped gift, said, 'You can relax, George, I don't think its a metal detector!' This crack earned him a laugh, and the Martian, with practised ease, passed smoothly into a series of amusing anecdotes, the topics of which ranged from presentation disasters to wildly inappropriate gifts.

Haskins had by this time convinced himself that the gift would indeed turn out to be a clock. It certainly didn't appear to be a deluxe chess set, which was just as well for he loathed the game; nor, for that matter, was it a toaster – at least he didn't think so.

The Martian lifted the package from the table. 'And now, folks, before I shut up and invite our honoured guest to open up, I'd like to add a few final remarks.' He half-turned towards the pallid-faced Haskins, paused for a few moments, heightening the sense of anticipation. 'You know, George,' he began, 'they say when a man retires that, strangely enough, his eyesight improves. He begins to see deeper and further, to make visual connections with things and events that until then had always appeared disparate and obscured by the grindstone dust. That's why I feel today most honoured to've been asked to present you with this thoroughly deserved retiral gift, one which we all hope will serve a symbolical as well as a practical role in the many days that lie ahead. Good birdhunting, George!'

Sangster's camera flashed as Haskins received the package and, tearing off its wrapping paper, revealed a bulky leather case, which he unzipped to expose a pair of deluxe binoculars.

The camera flashed again.

Having begun by saying that he was a man of few words, Haskins went on to prove this by delivering a one-minute speech in which he thanked them for such a wonderful and thoughtful gift. He also expressed his gratitude on behalf of his wife for the flowers, where-upon he abruptly concluded his address, taking his audience so much by surprise that their ragged applause sounded like a collective afterthought.

Rapidly the office began to empty. A few more folk came forward to shake his hand and to wish'm well, but the snipes left together without a word. Their newly-appointed leader, Mark Steeley, remained behind, possibly to see Haskins off the plant. With a friendly goodbye wave to Haskins, Conrad Bunston departed along with Mal Kibbley, who looked as if he expected to find a tumbrel waiting for'm outside.

As Haskins was thanking Beth Galton and Rose Renwick for their efforts on his behalf, Gerry Sangster approached him. 'Mr Haskins,' he began, 'd'you think you could oblige with just one more picture –'

Haskins shook his head. 'My skull's splitting as it is with that damned flash.'

Sangster resorted to his wheedling tone. 'Just the one – honest. You looking through those handsome bins. Make an arresting pic, Mr Haskins. "Former Security chief looks to the future" – something like that. One only. What d'you say?'

Haskins reluctantly agreed. 'Alright, but just the one,' he growled. 'Where d'you want me?'

Sangster led'm across to an office window, where he began to give him posing instructions. As Haskins complied, he was revelling in the sheer quality of the binoculars, marvelling at their amazing resolution, their lightness – the bins seemed to be floating in his grasp. Top of the range stuff – no doubt of it, the deluxe of the deluxe – not even his own headache-botched vision could lessen their obvious quality. A movement on MAD's roof apex took his glance: a finch of some kind was the best his dilapidated eyesight could suggest from this distance. But wait! Wasn't that a red flash? Ignoring Sangster's photo-prattle – 'Drop your right elbow a tad, will you!' – Haskins directed his distance-devouring glasses onto the roof target.

Glory be! And then there was light!

So close, so detailed he'd've sworn that the tiny creature was perched on the binoculars themselves. He'd lens-locked onto *Carduelis flammea cabaret*, the cheery little Common Lesser Redpoll. What absolute clarity of vision the powerful glasses were affording him. He could see distinctly the woodland bird's natty red cap, its fawn-brown face, black lores and bib, yellow bill, dark culmen and tip, pinkish breast flush suggesting a male of the species, black legs'n feet, wings were – Damn! With a flash of its scarlet head the bird suddenly vanished down the other side of the roof. At that moment, Sangster's camera tipped a brilliant splash of light over the ex-Supersnipe, startling him. Untrue to his promise, like most of the snapper tribe, he blatantly shutter-snatched four or five more shots of Haskins, the last two of which, ironically, would prove to be the most realistic studies of the former security supremo in the entire Haskins batch, depicting the true snarling, all but luminous rage of the irascible Supersnipe as he was best remembered by Centaur employees.

Having told Sangster that if he didn't stop poking his camera at'm, then his next shot would be a close-up of his anal passage – or words to that effect – Haskins swung his binoculars back to do a recce of the MAD rooftop. But the Lesser Redpoll'd gone.

A flash of yellow at ground level revealed itself in awe-inspiring detail to be Ratzo Runciman's van. Haskins frowned. What the devil was he doing stopped at a doorway that'd been blocked off ever since the MAD extension had rendered it obsolete? And a good thing too, since that particular entrance had always been a security blindspot.

His puzzlement increased when Ratzo came racing from his cab, flung open the van's back doors, then darted across to give the sealed door a couple of fist thumps. Almost immediately, the door partially opened and a car battery was passed out to Ratzo, which he hastily transferred to his van before returning to take hold of yet another battery. Suddenly the door was opened wider so that Haskins, with his enormously enhanced sight, was able to make out a figure in a grey coat overall, but the interior darkness obscured his face.

Ratzo took up a semi-crouching position and a tyre was rolled out t'm. No sooner had he hurled it into his van than another one was treated in similar fashion.

Haskins' heart began to pump harder. Was he for the first time actually witnessing a Magpie Operation? It was even possible that the shadowy figure in the demi-opened doorway was none other than The Magpie in person. By this time two more tyres had bounced into the pest-exterminator's van. Ratzo now returned to the door and soon had his arms filled with velour seat-covers, which he speedily transferred to his vehicle. A series of smaller items like car radios and clocks added to the booty.

Next on their shopping list were alternators (four of them), a couple of petrol tanks, and at least a dozen Salamander headlamps. An excited Haskins lowered his binoculars then swung around, expecting to find Steeley there. But only Jerry Sangster, gathering up his photographic gear, was present.

'D'you know where Steeley's gone?' he asked'm.

'To Hell in a wheelbarrow!' Sangster replied. He was obviously still sore about the way the ex-Super-snipe'd chewed'm up. Haskins glanced from the window. It was scarcely possible from this distance to make out with his mote-speckled vision whether the robbery was still in progress. He raised the binoculars to his eyes again. Yes, Ratzo was still loading up the van.

Sangster mumbled something.

'What's that?' asked Haskins.

'He's taking a leak.'

In the toilet Haskins' shout had an empty, echoing boom to it. He called again. Still no response. Then he remembered – the toilet, like the building itself, must now be obsolete. He hurried back to the old personnel main office and grabbed up a phone. The line was dead. He tried several others – same result. Snatching a quick glance through his binoculars, he saw Ratzo closing his van doors, securing them, then hurrying round to get into his cab.

Options for action were closing fast. He could run to the new personnel office and phone gate security from there; or he could check out its toilet for Steeley; better still, he could hot-foot it to the gatehouse itself to ensure that Runciman's van was thoroughly searched and not given the usual eye-tickle by officers who weren't all that keen to poke around amongst dead cockroaches, poisoned rats, and the pest-controller's pharmacopia of deadly chemicals. But he no longer had the authority to give anyone instructions; he was in a kind of industrial limbo, a hatless nonentity in a crumpled suit, a member of that impotent tribe of has-beens they branded with an 'Ex' before shipping them off to Zimmerland. But no way was he about to let this once-in-a-lifetime chance pass'm by. A groan escaped him as a further binocular recce confirmed that Ratzo's van was on the move. The groan, though, soon became a hiss of relief when he saw that the vehicle was heading away from the gate, making for, it appeared, the Dole Hole, the nickname given to a weed-infested area which was utilised as an auxiliary overspill storage space when room in the car-sales division was at a premium. This derelict piece of land, therefore, served as a rough indicator of the plant's industrial health.

A full Dole Hole was a worrisome sight for it obviously meant that Centaur Cars had begun to plummet in the auto-sales league, and, as a consequence, rumours of impending lay-offs became thicker on the ground than the proliferating rosebay, toadflax, and pineapple weeds in which the unwanted Sultans and Salamanders cooled their wheels.

Unaware that gaol rather than dole was looming over both him and his MAD accomplice (what a security coup it'd be should he turn out to be 'The Magpie'!), Runciman drove his van into the isolated piece of land, where no doubt he planned, unobserved, to stow the stolen gear further forward in his van, and cover it with tarps, sacking, crates, boxes, and anything else from the paraphernalia of his sordid trade that could provide concealment.

Peakham and Jowett were flabbergasted when they saw their former security chief come pelting towards the gatehouse, wagging a crackling bouquet of flowers as he ran, his eyes looking ripe to pop, and with a pair of encased binoculars bobbing on his chest.

'Like a stiff trying to catch up with his runaway hearse,' Jowett was later to describe'm.

Such a comical spectacle did he make, as he began to jabber a breathless tale about Ratzo Runciman . . . a sealed door that wasn't . . . binoculars . . . a bird on MAD's roof . . . Ratzo's van laden with spare car parts . . . large-scale theft . . . The Magpie . . . the Dole Hole . . . – that both guards found themselves oscillating between smirks and sniggers.

Jowett, in fact, was saved by the bell from outright laughter. His phone call lasted about a couple of minutes before he replaced the receiver and rejoined his partner and the panting, florid-faced Haskins. 'That was Steeley,' he said. 'Wondering where you'd gotten to.'

'Did you tell'm about Runciman, about me seeing the robbery through my binoc –'

'I told'm,' Jowett interrupted. 'He's alerting the West Gate in case Runciman tries to sneak out that way, and he's going to post a discreet surveillance on'm to make sure he doesn't get jumpy and try to dump his haul.' Jowett hitched his hat further forward on his head. 'He wants you to wait in your car, where he'll join you shortly. He reckons if Runciman spots you hanging around the gatehouse he'll smell a rat.'

This remark was the one that did the damage, causing Peakham's barely-checked laugh restraints to blow up'n his face like a trick cigar. His laughter – it sounded like a rhino in labour – had soon touched off a sort of whinnying response from his sidekick, who'd apparently just realised the comical aptness of his words.

'Be sure'n give Ratzo's van a good going-over, lads,' cautioned the former security supremo as he mopped pearls of sweat from his encrimsoned brow. His white hankie was so large and so extravagantly flourished that it seemed also to be serving as a flag of surrender, the abdication of his former, almost tyrannical authority.

Before the doom-burred prefix 'Ex' had so tenaciously battened onto his person, this pair of frisk virgins wouldn't have dared to laugh in his presence.

Haskins' neckbones crackled as he gave an emphatic nod. 'Yes, boys,' he urged, 'a rake-out from floor to roof, that's what's wanted.'

'Depend on us,' said Jowett. He nodded in the direction of the execs' carpark. 'All you gotta do is duck into your jalopy, and sit tight as a tick till Steeley joins you. Got that? Good. Off you pop, then.'

Patronising little sod! Spelling everything out like he was addressing a retarded ape . . . Bitterly conscious of being the object of their now unfettered laughter Haskins tramped across the yard. He unlocked his car and ducked inside. Thankfully, once he'd snapped the door shut he could no longer hear the derision from the gatehouse. He placed Dora's bouquet on the passenger seat, then, judging that Steeley'd want to sit there, he transferred the blooms to the rear cushions.

With a carefulness that verged on the reverential, Haskins unslung the encased binoculars from around his neck and stowed them in the glove compartment. Dora'd no doubt sum up her opinion of his presentation gift in two words: 'absolutely useless!' In a way, she'd be right, but, then, maybe not; it could well transpire that his birdwatching days were far from over. It all depended on Dora's depressed sister, Pearl, and whether she'd prove willing to extend her proposed holiday with them for at least the duration of the Twitcher Season. That Dora'd raise any objections seemed unlikely, for hadn't she that very morning voiced her misgivings about having him 'under her wheels all day'?

Haskins took some painkillers from his pocket and thumbed three of them loose from their protective foil. These he slammed into his panting mouth. At first the triple cluster became lodged in his gullet and a wave of panic and nausea swept through'm. This, however, soon passed as the quick-dissolving pills sank into his churning system.

Haskins settled back in his seat, then, closing his eyes, he spectated for a short while on an optical flea circus. (What astonishing acrobatics these jumping, leaping particles could perform!) Yawning now, he folded his arms across the steering wheel. He resisted the temptation to cradle his throbbing head on them . . . but, minutes later, he was angered to discover that not only had he succumbed to this desire but he'd compounded it by dozing off. Haskins gazed blearily across the yard at the gatehouse. Jowett was booking through a fuel tanker while his mate, Peakham, his arms casually folded, stood in the gatehouse doorway watching the procedure. Haskins relaxed. At least he hadn't missed the main action, the arrest of Ratzo Runciman, and, as a consequence, the possibility of The Magpie's capture. What a fantastic security coup that'd be! It was galling that Steeley'd bag all the credit (Haskins, having surrendered his industrial policing powers, fully recognised his bystander role in the imminent seizure of Runciman) but he'd no doubt that the crucial part played by him would eventually be acknowledged. If not, there'd still remain a bountiful measure of self-satisfaction that he – and he alone! – had been instrumental in bringing the pair of rogues to book.

Haskins continued to stare at Jowett as he dealt with the tanker, but it was a view that was restricted by what appeared to be a darkfall of black snowflakes. From this distance the guard looked like one of those tiny wind-powered figures to be seen in some gardens, either sawing furiously at a log, or, in golfer's guise, eternally swinging a club at an unbudgable ball. The silvery tanker, too, appeared so tiny it might've driven directly from Toyland.

Haskins knuckled his eyes, but when he opened them again the perspective distortions had, if anything, intensified. So far away and so shrunken did everything appear that it was like looking at the world through the wrong end of a telescope.

Hadn't Conrad Bunston claimed in his eloquent presentation speech that now he'd achieved retirement his vision would improve? Some improvement! But, to be fair, Bunston had been speaking metaphorically. With a deep yawn, Haskins slumped back in his seat. He felt utterly fatigued, so weary that he'd've sworn he could hear his very bones snoring. It must be the effect of the painkillers; he'd definitely exceeded the recommended dosage, but to no avail – the pills hadn't so much as dented his monolithic migraine.

His eyelids flickered shut. He could hear Dora's bouquet making rustling sounds, a sort of cellophane sibilance that suggested a floral conspiracy was afoot, a sinister murmuring on the very margins of hearing. With a forced cough he tried to overwhelm the bouquet's ghostly gossiping, but it continued unabated with its whisperings of christenings, weddings, and funerals.

Cautiously, Haskins peeled the upper lids from his flash-scorched eyes; the illusory black snowflakes were still falling, myriads of them, which, with all the dark zeal of a devil blowing out altar candles, attacked and expunged light wherever they encountered it. Through this optical murk, the squinting Haskins saw Steeley crossing the yard, but without so much as a glance in his direction or even a signal of some kind to indicate his awareness of the ex-Supersnipe's presence he vanished into the gatehouse.

Haskins glimpsed something red flashing across the windscreen. The object paused, hovered for some seconds, then alighted on the Sultan saloon's bonnet. It was the Common Lesser Redpoll!

It proved to be one of the happiest few moments Haskins had experienced in a long time. He sat there watching the dark brown little bird that hopped around so playfully, cocking its red skullcap and glancing inquisitively at its reflection in the bonnet's fiery shine. Haskins was convinced that the clowning creature had spotted him, for now'n again it hopped right up to the windshield and seemed to peer in at'm, then bounced off for some more leggy capering on the Sultan's bright lid, scolding him at the same time with its thin metallic twitterings.

With a nod, Haskins signified his endorsement of the Redpoll's bickering censure. Yes, indeed he did have more to do with his time than to sit here awaiting his petty moment of triumph. Pardon? Childish? Yes, he'd go along with that, too. But as it says in the Good Book, revenge is a powerfully sweet thing – sweeter even than honey, which was why he supposed that an old sourpuss like himself found it to be so damnably tempting.

But what of yourself, my feathered friend? Why're you winging around an ugly car plant, 'stead of being where you belong – perched on the jouncy branch of an old oak tree soaking up birdsong? The Redpoll, having ceased its twittering, took one last slide down the sloping bonnet, its comical black legs and feet duplicating themselves in the Warlord Red paint's high gloss. Its lively slapstick performance now over, the bird, like an old vaudeville trouper, began to take its bows, doing so with such a theatrical display of toadying gratitude that it would've come as no great surprise to the delighted Haskins had the zesty performer whipped off its jaunty red cap and waved it at'm before taking wing. But the clowning finch had something even more spectacular lined up for its grand finale. Bouncing breezily from its improvised scarlet skating rink, and lightly hurdling the bonnet-grille, it hooked its black spidery feet into the driver's wash-wiper then, using this as a support, it stared with a bold, impudent eye through the glass directly into the astonished Haskins' face. The twitcher being watched by the bird! But it wasn't finished, having yet one more trick in its repertoire; leaning still closer, it very distinctly rapped a half a dozen times on the wind-screen with its yellow bill before it detached itself and, with a ripple of metallic chatter, it soared away. Its flightpath took it across the yard and directly over the gatehouse pole-barrier, upon which it paused for a few moments, then was gone.

For the first time in ages, Haskins was whistling, well, not so much whistling as causing a series of thin notes to issue from his unpractised lips, which (who would've believed it!) were themselves seeking to master the mechanics of a smile. Despite the noise of his car's engine, from which he was provoking loud and extravagant growls, he went on with his warble prac-tice, even becoming ambitious enough to try'n coax out something that might be a recognisable tune from his stridulent mouth.

So swiftly did he reverse his Sultan from the ranks of gleaming, money-no-option models that he was only an inch or so from wing-clipping the Supreme Martian's Sapphire Blue Super Estate. He swung his car free from the élite auto-pack, then, like a dragster racer, surged towards the gatehouse and tyre-shrieked to a halt that was perilously close to the barrier-pole.

'What's all the hurry-hurry, George?'

The speaker was Steeley, who thrust his head into the window and rammed his face so close to Haskins' that they were almost touching. Steeley availed himself of a deep professional sniff before withdrawing slightly. 'Well, George,' he asked the strangely serene-looking Haskins, 'who tossed the squib in your tank, eh? You came from that auto pack burning more rubber than a fire in a condom factory.'

Behind him, the gatehouse duo, Jowett'nd Peakham, sniggered loudly. Instead of the expected scowl, something that looked remarkably like a smile was blooming on Haskins' lips.

He nodded towards the gatehouse guards. 'Tell either Stan'r Olly to hoist the Barber's Pole, will you?'

'I thought you'd want to see Runciman getting his collar felt,' Steeley said, then added. 'By the way, your info on the old MAD door was bang-on – it's been recently tampered with. If we nab Ratzo I'll see you get the credit – that's a promise.'

To his astonishment, Haskins was shaking his head. 'Forget it, son,' he said. 'You can have'm as a farewell present.' He revved the engine, shouting over its roars, 'I've gotta get going: I'm needed back home.'

'You get one of them new-fangled cordless phones then, George?'

Haskins shook his head.

'Then, how come,' the puzzled-looking new Super-snipe asked, as Jowett raised the pole-barrier, 'how come you know you're needed at home?'

'A little bird told me!' laughed Haskins. He eased off the handbrake, then, for the last time, with a jaunty-sounding farewell horn toot, he drove through Centaur's exit gate.

## A NIP IN THE AIR

You'll recall of course those
little yellow creeeps who recently dropped by to have a
good Nipponese sneer at our
primitive car making. The
news is that they've decided to red-card the remaind--
er of their Euro-Centaur
tour and are en-route to
Tokyo in a 'winged hospital'.
These battered and
bruised Banzai merchants
wont forget in a hurry their
visit to 'Broadmoor', where, led
by their militant shoppy, ,
'The Human Sardine' theops
gave the camera-clicking
plants pelters with 'metal
Unietti' and told them where
they could stick their cameras.
One son who wont be rising
for some time to come is the
leader of the delegation,
hara Tokugawa. Speaking
through an interpreter and
a mouthful of broken teeth
he said: that the ops spirited
response to their visit had
blot teahs of glatitude to
his eyes and a lump to his hloa
hloat, not to mention uzza
atz of his anatomy.' One

of Tokugawa's party is
said to be awaiting bowel
surgery - a Nikonectomy -
in the hope of revocering
his camera.
    Said a furious 'Martian':
'This was meant to be a bridge-
building exercis' Which
prompts the obvious question:
'Kwai bother?'

## RUN ROBOT RUN!

Greetings. Tin Heads, thisis
your Beloved Leader with a
special message for all of our
hard-working cardroids. Now, if
you'll take your noses from the
grindstone a sec... No, tell you
what, as-you-were with your
sniffers, but lets drop the vol
a tad on the auto shanties.
That's better. Rumours have
been circulating about our
plant's alleged policy changes
with regards to labour hire.
which discrininates against
cardroids in favour of humanoids. You have my pledge that
such is not the case. I dont
deny that 100 humanoids were
taken on at our Chimeford Plant

.but this will be on a casual
basis for the purpose of factory refurbishment. Your plume
jobs are safe, you have my
categorical assurance on that.
No humanoid will get as much
as a sniff at sceptic-tank
cleaning, gunge-removal, and
garbage disposal - such
tasks would belong soley to
cardroids in perpetuity. So,
lets have those smiles back
on your interfaces. And lets
hear our slogan loud'n clear -
Altogether: 'When the Centaur
is galloping/The Japs take a
walloping' Excellent. Now,
back to your palces and all
that sparky stuff you do so
  well!

# The
# Day
# the
# Bad News
# Came

How The Human Sardine had come by his nickname
was anybody's guess. One theory claimed that the
soubriquet was the militant shoppy's own invention, a
means by which he'd dodged more obvious epithets
such as Bandy or Cowboy. Although the slight curva-
ture of his pins remained, the sheer novelty of his
nickname and the continuing speculation as to how he
might've acquired it had succeeded in diverting the
attention of his co-workers from his lower limbs and
added an exotic gloss to his notoriety for being the
most gung-ho of Centaur's senior stewards, not only in
Broadmoor, his home base, but plant-wide.

On the day the bad news came, or to be strictly
accurate, on the morning of that dire day, The Human
Sardine was – surprise! surprise! – trying to hold the
floor at a specially convened JRC meeting by juggling

more rhetorical balls than even he was capable of handling, and spouting more character condemnations than a hanging judge on speed.

But if ears, like eyes, had lids, then the twenty pairs of listeners The Human Sardine was seeking to penetrate would've been well'nd truly shuttered. Anyway, at the top of the lengthy rectangular table, around which the bulk of the senior shoppies were seated while the remainder sat along the green, gloss-painted walls, a pair of empty seats were creating such a silent uproar that they'd all but succeeded in drowning out The Sardine's bellicose braying.

Waving a copy of the KIKBAK, The Human Sardine was directing his fury at O'Hara, who was widely believed to've been the founder of The Laffing Anarkists, a political grouping much distrusted by Centaur's Marxists, Trots, and Maoists, not to mention a scattering of lesser lefties.

This public attack on both himself and what his antagonist vindictively referred to as his 'industrial *Beano*' appeared not to be fazing O'Hara in the slightest: he just sat there, having a puff, letting smoke drift through his gappy teeth.

The KIKBAK's pages crackled as The Human Sardine continued to wave it around.

'Are you saying,' he asked, 'that this crap's the best you could do for Curly? I mean, a man's job was at stake – his very livelihood – not to mention his reputation, and what do you come up with? A warning to the Martians maybe? A threat that any attempt to dismiss Brother Brogan on a trumped-up charge of theft would trigger massive and immediate industrial action from every hourly-paid op in the plant?'

He began to ruffle through the KIKBAK's pages. 'Maybe I missed it. I just can't believe a macho outfit like yours would've passed up the chance to kick them Martian's green arses . . .'

The Human Sardine gave up his pantomime search, then, shaking his head, he sighed aloud. 'Nope. It seems our giggling goons've shat it and are now more interested in the new Supersnipe, who on the first week of his job bagged a "bug buster" and just missed out on capturing The Magpie. Shouldn't surprise us none. For haven't we always suspected that when the chips're down your average Laffing Anarkist is about as good at waging war as he is at spelling?'

This crack won The Sardine a hearty laugh, and some of the stewards pummeled the table top with their fists to signify their approval. But O'Hara merely grinned and tapped some cig ash into an empty plastic coffee cup.

Riding a favourable tide, The Human Sardine pressed home his attack. 'Yeah, the Martians can rest easy – they've nothing to fear from this comic. In fact, I can see only one use for it.' The Sardine got to his feet then, turning his rear to the table, he began to wipe his backside with the KIKBAK. Next, finger-pinching his nostrils, he mimed the flushing of a lavvy pan before crumpling the mag into the ball and tossing it over his shoulder in the direction of the still totally unfazed O'Hara. But his aim proved abortive; the balled KIKBAK bounced across the polished tabletop and lodged itself in the crook of Tantamount Oslake's folded arms. Affronted-looking, the shoppy hastily plucked the mag from his person and with a disdainful sweep of his hand cuffed the KIKBAK onto its intended target.

By this action he was evidently anxious to convey the sense of revulsion that Laffing Anarkism aroused in him, and clearly to show that the hallmark of his stewardship: 'A little Moderation avoids much Botheration!' hadn't been compromised.

'It's official then, is it?' asked Alf Double Cross. 'Curly's definitely got the bullet?'

The Human Sardine confirmed this with a tight little nod.

'That's a diabolical liberty!' Cross snapped. 'A fuck'n set-up if ever there was one.'

The Human Sardine looked miffed now that Cross had pinched his spotlight.

'I suppose the buggers've charged'm?' enquired Cross.

'Only if he carries out his threat to kick up a stink to his MP and the tabloids 'bout how them Nippleheads cut up rough with his invalid mother, and trashed his flat so badly it looked like a Panzer division had stormed through it – twice!'

'Curly'd find that tough sledging,' put in Walt Struthers, a paint shop rep.' He smirked. 'Not kicking up a stink, I mean.'

This remark, to The Human Sardine's chagrin, deflected attention from O'Hara, and further wisecracks about the former steward's almost phobic fear of soap'n water made a return to his attack on the KIKBAK and its founder a lost cause.

Tommy Farr, a seat section steward, wanted to know if the extraordinary meeting concerned Curly Brogan's dismissal. The Human Sardine vetoed this speculation. Shaking his head, he said that he doubted if Brother Brogan's unfair and obviously engineered sacking would've prompted the Martians to've also called for the attendance of the Staff Union leaders of both the shopfloor and the office structures. He'd also heard a strong rumour, The Sardine told the murmuring stewards, that the Centaur had alerted the Press to stand by for an important Company statement.

'Whaja think's on the go, then?' Farr persisted with his questioning. 'A nightshift knock-off, maybe?'

The Human Sardine shrugged his shoulders. 'Could be! We've had three track-speed cuts; there's over a hundred ops in the Labour Pool, and the Dole Hole's jam-packed.' He shook his head. 'I hope I'm wrong, but these three facts alone suggest that the Martians aren't about to announce a wage rise.'

The babble of voices got louder in the smoky room, but at the far end of the table the two empty chairs maintained their deafening silence. Not for long. The door opened. Two men entered, namely, Bill Bascome, the hourly-paids' Convenor, and Jim Grant, his deputy. Both of them looked deeply unhappy. In a silence no less profound they seated themselves at the table. Bascombe, who'd entered carrying a sheet of paper which bore the Centaur logo, laid it on the table and flattened out its creases with his hand. Next, he reached into an inner pocket and produced his glasses. Before he put them on he muttered something to his grim-faced deputy, then got slowly to his feet.

He cleared a mucousy frog from his throat but seemed to've replaced it with a catarrhal toad, so thick was his voice, so low'nd emotional that it proved difficult for his audience to make'm out at first – something about'm being the 'wearer of black shoes', was it? No, course not – 'The bearer of bad news'. Yeah, that was it. The stewards braced themselves. So too did their Convenor. He drew a deep, shuddering breath, then, haltingly, out it came, the unbelievable sentence that transformed them from men of substance into factory wraiths: 'Lads, they've pulled the plug on us; they've decided to shut down the whole plant; everything's to go – lock, stock'n barrel. The whole shebang!'

In the silence a voice, Oslake's, came trembling forth: 'B-but they c-can't do that. Not the entire plant. Why, that's tantamount to industrial homicide . . .'

Bascombe nodded in agreement, then, slipping on his specs, he lifted the sheet of paper from the tabletop, and, once again clearing his throat, said: 'I'll now read the Company's Statement . . .'

### BRING ME THE HEAD OF DON SCIFFIONI!

A horrific accident happened in MAD, Friday last, when greyback
Don Sciffioni, strayed into a "working area" and was promptly
dismembered by Frankie Faggleton's forky truck.

Although it seened a lost cause " king Prawn" , the
section's first-aider, decided to chance his hand at some
"rude surgery" . There was no doubting it, when it came to
crude, primitive scalpery, Prawn was the foremost in his field.
Certainly, he was a specialist in rudeness. "Right, saggy tits"
he snarledat his female assistant,Polly Pottles, "make with
5cc's of effin medroxyprogesterne acetate; 2 cc's of promethazie
theoclate;and a glass of water for the patient". "Hadn't we best
wait until they've found his head? asked Pottles.

Prawn, who'd only just finishing instructing an op on the art
of mallet-induced anaesthesia, turned angrily on his assistant.
" don't be so damned cautious," he snarled at'r.. You'll always
be a foutth-aider with all your nitpickery.

Pottles shook'r head. "It just seems Crazy, operating on a
decapitce,"

" There you go again with your neg vibes!" Prawn shook his
head. "Why should Doc 'Mengeles' always get the juicy stiff
while talented first-aiders like myself get lumbered with nickel'nd
dime amputations?"

"But"protested Pottles, " what can be done for a headless
patient?" .

" The head'll turn up. You'll see..." No sooner'd Prawn
said this than an op came running inot the section dribbling a
head. " O ye of little faith!" bellowed a triumphant"King"
Prawn. He snatched the head from the op who'd begun to play
keep-uppy with it, and lobbed it to Pottles. "right", Glumchops
- get weaving!"

" I can't," Pottles protested.

" Course you can," Prawn assured her. "I know it sounds a bit
dunting, but after the first thousand sutures it's all downskull."
   " It's not that..."
   " What then?"
   "The head - it's not Don Sciffioni's!"
   " You're crazy! It's got to be"
   " Well it aint. Not unless before that forky scattered'm
he changed gender,not to mention colour."
   "it's bound to've suffered some damage. I mean when you---
   "Quit the bullshitry" snapped Pottles. "It's an African
negress's head!" At that moment the op-cum-anaesthetist put
Prawn to sleep with a skillful mallet blow. Meanwhile lodged in
a high roof stnchion the missing head of Don Sciffioni hummed:
" Ciâo, Ciao, Bambino!..."

                ***********************

# Ending

On that final morning the sequencers'd been
instructed by their gaffer, Stan Cutter, to foregather in
the telex shack. In ones and twos they did so, most of
them arriving with steamy cups of coffee. Sam Gates
and Steve Laker, the telex ops, had naturally claimed
their right to the most comfortable chairs while the rest
made do with plastic 'bum-bruisers' or makeshift seats
contrived from boxes of telex paper rolls. Since Steve
Laker'nd Biggles Blane were the only non-smokers in
the squad it proved fortunate that the roof of the telex
shack (otherwise known as The Rabbit Hutch) consisted of a wire-mesh covering, thereby providing an
escape route for the cigarette smoke as well as an
emergency exit for a wasp. This Made-In-Hell winged
beastie had been on a solo mission, scouting for
something stingable. Buzzing through the trim shop

it'd come upon what looked like a bombed henhouse and, upon descending to check it out, it discovered that this industrial hovel was chockablock with its prime enemy – the Swatteroos!

Fearlessly, the wasp'd begun to dive-bomb them, but it'd soon realised it'd been lured into an ambush when the hateful human bipeds had, en masse, simultaneously, whipped out their anti-wasp terror weapon – the rolled-up newspaper! The stinger did not linger, but, gamely dodging the press flak, soared to safety through the roof.

The phone rang.

'Hold the trapdoor!' shouted Tommy Small, the squad's veteran. 'It might be a reprieve!'

Sam Gates let the phone ring for a full minute longer before he picked up the receiver. 'Yeah? Stalag 17.'

Gates looked bored by what his line-sharer had to say. He yawned loudly into the mouthpiece. 'Right. Got that. Sorry, say again? How many what're here? Sequencers?' Gates began to count the plastic coffee cups that flecked the wire mesh roof. 'At a rough guess I'd say around seven or maybe even eight. Kinda hard to be exact with'm milling around. What's that? Their names?' Gates shook his head. 'Sorry – no can do. Why not? Coz I don't feel like it – okay? Tell you what – why don't you get off your cobwebbed arse and come down here'n count'm yourself?'

Amidst gasps and uneasy glances, Gates chucked down the receiver. 'That,' he told them, 'was our Big Effendi. He thought we'd like to know that we're due to "get done" at 11 a.m. precisely. And, don't forget, even if you're only a teensy-weensy bit late you'll miss out on your FREE balloon and comic.'

Gates glanced through the dusty window pane, which, now that the model-storage lines had been cleared, provided'm with an unrestricted view of the bare trim shop up to and beyond Cutter's tiny office. As he continued to watch he saw Cutter leaving the office and heading their way.

'Here he comes, lads,' said Gates. 'And if you ask me he don't look too happy 'bout something.'

Halfway down the trim shop, Ernie Bolton, a fitter, who'd been ripping up floor-rails, began, as the wrathful-looking Senior Sequencer drew near'm, to behave in a bizarre fashion. To look at'm, as he leapt suddenly to his feet, and began to jig'nd jive around, his arms flapping, hands flailing, you'd've thought Bolton'd been striken by yon medieval dance mania. What'd it been called again? Gates's brow wrinkled. Saint something, was it? Yeah – Vitus, St Vitus's Dance. Its victims, apparently, cavorted in a non-stop frenzy, much like Little Richard on Bennies.

It seemed, however, that the contemporary St Vitus's Dance was extremely short-lived though rapidly contagious, for Bolton's joyless jig suddenly ceased, as did his facial contortions, and his writhing arms and flapping hands began to settle like the vanes of a becalmed windmill. It was now Dan Laverty, Bolton's mate's turn to manifest the symptoms of the St Vitus-like affliction, only he demonstrated wilder limb-threshing, so much so that the cotton rag fluttering in his grasp made'm look like a manic Morris dancer.

Once again the symptoms proved ephemeral, and Laverty, like Bolton, swiftly returned to normal. Cutter, who'd watched both men's weird performances with growing alarm, now appeared anxious to distance himself from them. His pace, that'd already been fast, became even more rapid but it seemed that he wasn't quite speedy enough: the plague, St Vitus's Dance, or whatever it was that induced the grotesquely comic effect of a man who appeared to be wrestling himself, or with flying hands spun like a Dervish, had now caught up with the Senior Sequencer, robbing him entirely of even a modicum of authority.

Adding insult to invisible injury, or so it seemed, Tommy Small dashed from the telex shack and struck his gaffer a brisk blow on his left shoulder with a rolled-up newspaper: a wasp, yet another casualty in the ceaseless strife between man and insect, dropped to the floor, writhed for a few seconds, then was still.

'Thanks,' said the ruffled-looking Cutter. 'Can't stand those bastards.'

Small shrugged, but said nothing. The look of sheer terror on the Senior Sequencer's face as the striped demon had buzzed him was a sight not to be forgotten by his squad. Instead of leaving things as they were, Cutter, whose badly stung and inflamed ego made'm ultra-sensitive to the men's scarcely concealed smirks, tried to restore what he thought of as his 'air of authority' by crassly giving them an order. Having jotted the names of those present into his 'staff book', he snapped it shut, then in his hoarse voice addressed the sequencers: 'I want you to stay put – that means remain here. Right? No buggering off anywhere. Got that?'

If the men had in fact 'got that' then going by their glowers they didn't much want it. In fact, Steve Laker channelled his resentment into action by rising to his feet and zipping up his anorak. Next, he stepped through the snack's doorway and brushed past the edgy-looking Cutter. 'I'm for some fresh air,' he said.

'Me as well.' Sam Gates rose and followed his telex partner past the Senior Sequencer.

'Wait for me, lads!' Tom Small'd joined the absconders and was followed by the rest of the squad. As the men streamed past'm Cutter wisely decided against doing his King Canute. Instead, he shouted what was probably a husky-voiced warning. Whatever it was it went unheeded by the sequencers, who'd now fragmented into groups of two'nd three and had gone on defiant walkabout.

'What an asshole,' said Gates. He was walking between Laker and Small. 'You'd think to hear'm that he wasn't getting the chop like the rest of us.'

They strolled into the body'n white, where Gates and Small joined the queue at the tea'nd coffee dispenser. Laker drifted in the direction of the snack area, where a rowdy card game was reaching its climax. On his way there he'd passed ops dressed in their civvies who were stripping their lockers, while others involved themselves in a tea-mug-smashing ceremony. As Laker approached the gambling school the session had just concluded. To signify this the dealer, with a loud whoop, lobbed the card deck into the air; for a second or so the cards seemed to hang on the levitating cigarette smoke before they fell with a multi-suited rattling on the table, the floor, and upon the gamblers themselves: clubs, spades, diamonds, and heavy, heavy hearts.

'Hey, Spunky,' one of'm shouted to the passing op, 'are you going to the dance?'

Spunky paused. 'What dance?'

'The Redun-Dance!' the ops roared in unison, then rolled about laughing as if the joke'd been freshly minted.

Laker rejoined Sam Gates and Tom Small and they made their way along the passageways formed by cratefuls of metal stampings. So unnaturally quiet was it that Laker had the odd feeling that they were leaving footprints on the silence.

'Y'know, I still find it hard to accept – the Yanks dumping us like that.' The speaker was Tom Small. He took a sip of coffee. 'The nightshift getting the kibosh – a blind man could've seen that coming. Always on the cards it was. But the whole shooting match.' He shook his head. 'No, I never thought it'd come to that – not'n a thousand years.'

'What threw me,' said Steve Laker, 'was how we consistently kept meeting our production targets during the ninety-day run-down. Place ran like clockwork.'

Gates nodded. 'There's nothing like a "golden handshake" to curb militancy. A grand-in-the-hand's better than two feet in a picket line.'

'What makes it more galling's those dagos hijacking our car,' Small observed. 'I mean, it was taken for granted that with the Sultan Saloon entering its fourth series the Centaur Cascade was a cert to be built here.'

'That's what comes of counting your autos before they're hatchbacks,' quipped Gates. 'Tell me this,' he now said, 'if you were sitting in Detroit and comparing our production record against Centaur Bilbao, to which plant would you send the "Gate Slammers": the one that rarely "hits the cobbles" and that would've exceeded its sales target if it hadn't been unlucky enough to get lumbered with duff brake components, forcing it to recall its best-selling model? Or would you favour Centaur Chimeford, with our notoriously militant trade unions and bolshie labour force, not forgetting the cowardly act of appeasement that denied us an engine-build plant and as a result meant we'd to ship our supplies from as far away as Coventry? Add to that planning blunder Chimeford's over-reliance on independent components suppliers – it's no contest.'

They emerged from the silent and gloomy building and were immediately confronted by an even more depressing sight – Tombstone Telfer, well known for his stern, authoritative manner, was to be seen openly sobbing while a pair of his colleagues sought to comfort him.

'Hup-two-three-four, hup-hup-hup . . .'

A group of overalled punters, led by their greyback, came marching through a doorway. Of all the events he'd witnessed that morning, from the wasp attack, the squad's disregard of Cutter's instructions, the gamblers playing it for laughs in dire circumstances, the weeping redneck, the image of those marching punters etched itself the most deeply on Laker's memory.

'Hup-two-three-four, hup-hup-hup . . .'

Applause from rednecks, greybacks, operators, and staff accompanied them all by the way to the exit gate.

Laker glanced at his watch. It was almost time to do that far far better thing . . . a Datsun saloon drew up alongside them. Its driver, a pal of Tom Small's, offered them a lift to the South Side office, where the severances would take place. The trio declined. It was bad enough being branded an industrial 'shake-out' by Madame Thatcher without hitching a ride to the Killing Place in a Japanese tumbrel.